HIXON

A CLYDEN'S RANCH WISEGUYS NOVELLA

By Esther E. Schmidt

THE CLYDEN'S RANCH

Copyright © 2023 by Esther E. Schmidt All rights reserved.

No part of this book may be reproduced in any form, without permission in writing from the author.

This book is a work of fiction. Incidents, names, places, characters and other stuff mentioned in this book is the results of the author's imagination. The Clyden's Ranch is a work of fiction. If there is any resemblance, it is entirely coincidental.

This content is for mature audiences only. Please do not read if sexual situations, violence and explicit language offends you.

Cover design by:
Esther E. Schmidt

Editor #1:
Christi Durbin

Editor #2:
Virginia Tesi Carey

Cover Model:
Kevin R Davis

Photographer:
JW Photography / Jean Woodfin

CHAPTER 01

HIXON

I fill my lungs with fresh, clean air and let my gaze roam over the pastures that now belong to me. No matter the day or time, worries or workload, this is what it's all about. Nature always gives me a sense of serenity, but the feeling of accomplishment as I take in my surroundings also satisfies the restlessness in my bones.

This ranch is located in a little town in Montana and was founded by my father many decades ago. It's the only home I've known. Even if I've spent years living in another state with my ex-wife, trying to fit in for the kids' sake. The one thing we all learned from those years is the fact that you shouldn't force anyone to "fit in." It's suffocating and creates a toxic environment for everyone involved.

The best decision I ever made is coming back to

this place, bringing my two sons along with me. Sons who their mother never gave two shits about. Except for the picture sitting on her desk to make it seem like she's human and not the cold-ass workaholic who doesn't care about anything else but her pristine career.

"Pissed off at the crack of sunrise. Great start to the day." Shepherd chuckles and I turn my head to glare at my oldest son.

Twenty-four-years-old and still a royal pain in my ass. Both my sons have returned to the ranch after their time spent in the military and the careers they pursued to join my line of work. The ranch is big enough and we each have a part of it, so we don't have to run into one another.

Between the ranch and our whiskey distillery, along with the consultancy assignments we take for the government, it's a lot of work. This is also the reason why we're hiring someone to help take care of our horses so we can focus on other things.

"I don't like hiring new people. Especially not when it involves having them live here as well," I tell Shepherd, also the truth but the kid doesn't need to know my pissed off look was because I reminded myself of his mother.

My sons suffered enough with the lack of love and attention from her side. Thank fuck my mother at least made up for my ex-wife's flaws and helped me raise them.

"It's necessary. You turned down the first few

who showed up for the job without letting them say one damn word. Try not to scare the next two away who will hopefully show up later today." Shepherd shakes his head. "Which reminds me. Did you contact the potential buyer for the black mare?"

"I did. He's picking her up on Friday. I'm going to let Romer handle it, he's the one who trained her."

Shepherd winces. "He's not going to like it."

"The very reason he needs to handle it. That boy wants to keep all the damn horses," I grumble.

The corner of his lips twitch. "Twenty-two is hardly a boy."

I stroke my gray beard. "He's still wet behind the ears, and so are you."

"I'm a man, Dad," he proudly states and shoots me a smirk as he spurs on his horse and speeds away.

"I'm a man," I echo in a mocking tone and snort. "Says the boy who just tried to race home the way he's been doing ever since he could ride." I slowly shake my head. "Boys will be boys."

Releasing a deep breath, I spur Witness on, my twelve-year-old Gypsy Cob. She was born and bred on this ranch and I've trained her myself. It's also why I named her Witness 'cause the damn horse has been following me around ever since she was born.

I love this breed. My father founded this ranch and bought a Gypsy Cob stallion along with two mares. He never stopped working, breeding, and training till he was forced to blow out his last breath three weeks ago. Every inch of this land is covered with his blood, sweat, tears, and love and it fucking shows.

And now it's all mine. Mine and my sons to continue breeding these magnificent horses. Along with the whiskey that started out as a private stash for me and my old man around ten years ago, but quickly evolved to a cash flow neither of us expected.

I'm holding the reins in one hand and the other I keep away from my body as the seventeen hundred pound animal underneath me catches up to Shepherd's horse. The sharp wind hits me in the face, movement of the powerful beast below me, along with everything else gives me the rush I love when it comes to ranch life. It temporarily blocks out all the turmoil inside my head.

The best of more than one world where we combine family, breeding horses, making whiskey, and working cases; doing all the things we enjoy without any restrictions. Shepherd and I both lean back and bring our horses to a stop when we notice Romer stalking toward a truck that just drove through the open gates and is now parking in front of the main house.

"Are we expecting anyone?" I rumble as I dismount and let my boots hit the dirt and gravel.

Shepherd is already standing next to his horse and shrugs. "I don't think so. The two interviews we have planned for hired help are scheduled for later today."

I hand him the reins. "Take care of Witness and

I'll handle this."

The corner of his mouth twitches. "By handling, you mean run them off."

Ignoring him I stomp toward the truck and notice Romer bracing his arm against the vehicle's door and bobbing his head to whatever the driver is asking him. Romer steps back and the door opens, revealing a curvy dark-haired woman.

Her side profile is enough to make my cock twitch behind the zipper of my jeans but when her blue eyes connect with mine? Fuck. Pure lust fills my veins and it's been years…hell, decades for such a raw craving to hit me full force. Come to think of it, I don't think I've ever experienced it this overwhelming and it's throwing me off-balance.

"Ah, here he comes now," Romer states. "I'm sure he has time to squeeze in an interview."

An interview? What the hell is he talking about? Oh, hell no. There is no way I can allow a woman to work here, let alone take a job that requires her to live in the same damn house as me. Dammit. She looks way younger than me but older than my boys. I'd say I have at least a decade on her.

I come to a stop in front of my youngest son and shoot him an annoyed glare–the one reflecting no bullshit which I've used in my time as a drill sergeant many years ago–and snap, "Shepherd needs your help in the stables."

He looks startled for a fragment of a second and I raise my eyebrow in challenge. He bobs his head and excuses himself to the woman before jogging off.

"Do you put the fear of hell in all your personnel? If so, I might rethink applying for the–"

"There is no job. And at this moment I don't consider him personnel," I growl, cutting off what she was about to say. "Neither do I think it's any of your damn business. This is private property. Leave."

She frowns and slams her door shut. Taking a step in my direction she tells me, "Tony Hay mentioned your ranch was looking for hired help concerning the horses. That boy you just ran off affirmed it as well. Do you have a problem with me? I have lots of experience and have references you can check."

One of her eyebrows shoots in the direction of the clear blue Montana sky, probably to challenge me, but it only makes my cock twitch inside my pants. Good thing she's still looking me in the eye and is oblivious to my attraction to her. I can't help but snort at her mentioning Romer being a boy. She doesn't seem much older than he is.

"I don't think you'll be a good fit. An interview would waste both our time and there's enough to do around here," I snap.

She purses her full lips, drawing my attention to the rose-colored plumpness I wouldn't mind seeing wrapped around my cock. Shit. Yeah, there's no way I can have her work around here, no matter how badly we need the help.

Dismissing her, I turn, but the feel of a soft hand

being placed on my inked forearm causes sparks of electricity to shoot straight to my dick. An explosion of emotion hits my chest and I rumble a low growl deep in my throat. I whirl around and crowd her space, forcing her to walk backward until her back hits her truck.

She stares up at me with wide eyes but they are not filled with fear. The dilated pupils, short gasps of air flowing from her parted lips, along with the rise and fall of her massive tits is the indication of one very aroused woman.

It would be easy and welcomed to lean in and taste her, but I'm too damn old to get caught up in anything that involves long- or short-term commitment. I have enough on my plate as it is when it comes to the ranch, the whiskey business, and the unexplained death of my father.

"What's going on?" I hear Shepherd's voice, which instantly rips the connection this woman and I were pulled into.

Taking a step back I snap, "Nothing. She was just leaving."

At the same time, the woman says, "I came for the job of ranch help."

"Great." Shepherd shoulders me aside and holds out his hand for her to take. "Shepherd Clyden. You've met my younger brother, Romer, and this grumpy old man is my father, Hixon. Come, let's go inside for some coffee and a chat."

She gives him a warm smile. "I'd love to. I'm

Clover Sterling."

Her eyes lock on mine over Shepherd's shoulder and her pouty lips slide into a smirk, basically giving me the finger as she follows him into the main house. If she thinks she has a shot at the job or can get a way in by charming my son, she's sadly mistaken.

I stomp into the house after them and am about to demand she leave when the door behind me opens and slams shut. Whirling around, I face Romer and the kid has the nerve to mutter, "Glad she made it inside," as he rushes past me. What the actual fuck?

"What made you come here to apply for the job?" I hear Shepherd ask as he starts to make a new pot of coffee.

Romer takes a few mugs out of the cabinet and places them on the kitchen table as if we're having a damn family meeting. I have no idea why the thought of a woman–especially this one–in my kitchen is making me feel on edge, but it simply does. I want to snarl at her to leave, yet I grit my teeth to hear her answer the question Shepherd just threw at her.

"To be honest? The chance to work with everything that involves horses all day, but also room and board is something I need right now. My boyfriend…well, ex-boyfriend as of this morning. He threw me out and I basically have one box of belongings in the back of my truck and nowhere to go." Her shoulders sag. "Sorry. I don't mean to sound broken and desperate. I could stay a few nights at my parents' ranch. Five days to be exact and then it won't belong to them anymore. A few months ago, they decided to sell everything and move to Italy. My father's side of the family lives there and with my mother's health it's better for her bones to have a warmer climate." Her smile is bright and loving when she adds, "Dad might also be homesick because it's his hometown they are moving to, but my brother is also there with his wife and my niece and nephew. I think they just want to enjoy being grandparents for longer than the handful of visits a year."

I grit my teeth at the mention of her ex-boyfriend and her family leaving her. My gut clenches and again I wonder why this woman affects me the way she does.

"We don't need you," I grunt. "We don't have the patience or can afford the drama you'll bring along for those couple of days it will take for either you or your boyfriend to come crawling back to one another."

The woman visibly winces. "No crawling back when you catch the man you gave four years of your life to fucking someone a decade younger. He didn't even stop." Her nose wrinkles. "He laughed right in my face and told me my old cunt was wider than a trash can and smelled similar, so it was time to trade me in."

Silence overtakes the room as my sons and I stare at her. What the fuck is wrong with some people?

She clears her throat and holds up the mug Romer placed in front of her. "Is the coffee ready? I sure could use some. And I swear that's the only drama you'll hear from me. It's time to put everything behind me and give myself a clean, fresh start. Like I said, my parents owned a ranch and I grew up with and have cared for horses all my life. My father loves the breed Anglo-Arabo Sardo and is taking the two last horses he still had with him. Quite the difference from those Gypsy Cobs I saw you guys riding."

I release a deep sigh and step toward the counter to grab the coffee pot.

Filling her mug I tell her, "If you don't do the work or so much as fucking annoy me, you'll be out on your ass faster than your legs can carry you."

Her whole face lights up. "Thanks so much. You won't regret hiring me. I love working with horses and am aware of everything that's needed to done around a ranch. I'm also an early riser and work hard. Any other rules I need to be aware of?"

I'm already regretting my decision and find myself saying, "Wear normal clothes around the house, no naked shit or flirting or having sex with my sons."

She snorts. "I'm way older so that's a given. Sorry, guys."

Both my boys chuckle but I keep staring at her, not getting the joke because I wasn't fucking kidding.

A glint of mischief dances in her eyes when she says, "So, flirting is still a go when it involves you?"

I mutter a curse and rub a hand over my face while my boys laugh their asses off. I knew this woman was trouble the moment her truck drove through the gates. And I'm already regretting my decision to hire her.

A Clyden's Ranch Wiseguys novella

CHAPTER 02

CLOVER

"You can find the schedule in the kitchen. It's a pretty standard rotation, but I guess your name will be added to the routine now. Breakfast and lunch are whatever you can grab by yourself. Dinner is made by my father three times a week and Romer and I also take a day, but we pick up some takeout on the weekends. Maybe that'll change now that you're here, but I don't think my father will cook less, he loves spending time in the kitchen, just like my grandma used to do. She was Italian and taught her son everything she knew. That woman could sure cook. My Dad too for that matter," Shepherd rattles and I haven't stopped smiling since I teased his father in the kitchen.

"Sounds familiar. I was born in Italy, but my parents moved here when I was ten. My mother also taught me everything there is to know and needless to say, I love baking and cooking as well. I can definitely help out. Maybe I can do breakfast to compensate? I'm an early riser so it's no big deal," I offer.

Romer bobs his head as we stroll into the stables. "Sounds perfect to me. I'll let Dad know when he gets back."

So strange to hear these grown men talk about their dad, Hixon. The grayish beard and the crinkles around the eyes show the man is older than me. I shouldn't be lusting after their father. Hell, I was just dumped and ended a four-year-old relationship due to cheating so why am I even attracted to him?

It's a good thing Hixon left right after I teased him about the flirting. Which wasn't actually teasing since there was some truth to it. Hixon muttered something about needing to call Hay for a reference. If my credentials checked out, I could move my stuff into the house. He left and that's when Shepherd and Romer offered to give me a grand tour of the ranch.

We weren't even out the door when Shepherd got a call from his father to let him know Hay spoke very highly of me and my parents. Hay supplies hay–what's in a name, right?–and other supplies a ranch needs and is acquainted with a lot of people throughout the state. Good thing too because he gave me this opportunity by letting me know the Clyden ranch was looking for hired help.

This morning I wasn't sure about a roof over my head let alone a job. My bank account and savings could hold me over for a few months, but life is expensive. Especially when I have no other choice but to live in a hotel. None of those worries are mine now. It was a bit of a risk to take the long drive here but definitely worth it in the end.

There are no issues clouding my mind other than remembering what my new tasks are and finding the routine these three men have going on around this ranch. I should feel heartbroken, catching my ex the way I did, but strangely enough, it feels more like I dodged a bullet. Even if the man cost me four years of my life.

You might say there were two to blame in this relationship going wrong. The slope of living alongside one another instead of with one another. I simply didn't care anymore or put the effort into everyday things. I felt more annoyed when he was home and in reality, he never was a loving man to begin with.

Maybe he wanted me to catch him cheating because my father terminated his job last month with them moving out of the country. Maybe my ex saw it as a chance to ditch me as well, who knows? It sure fits the timing with my parents leaving the country. In the end, nothing matters; it's locked in my past and I have to move forward.

Romer and Shepherd are done giving me a tour of the stables. They have one stallion, four mares, and two foals. They have one more mare, but Shepherd just told me they are selling her in a day or two. Romer mentioned he'd be in the stables tomorrow morning around seven and I could help with the routine for the horses.

I'm thankful for both of them. They seem sweet and have the patience to show me around and answer my questions. Unlike their father who gives me the impression he's a grump for more than one reason. I have yet to find those reasons.

Romer excuses himself and heads toward the house while Shepherd leads me to a large building located near the stables. "Next to breeding and training Gypsy Cobs we also own and run a small family distillery which was founded by my grandfather for his personal stash."

I completely ignore Shepherd as I step inside the building and take in the tall gleaming columns in the large space. "Wow," I whisper in awe.

"Come on, let's skip to the good part," Shepherd tells me and guides me to stairs that lead to a basement.

He hits a light switch and exposes the barrels horizontally stored three high on racks.

"There's no artificial climate control." He grins. "The fluctuation of the temperature causes the liquid to expand and contract, which in return cause the whiskey to drive into the wood." He points at the rack near the floor. "Those mature at a more consistent temperature—"

I'm staring at him with keen interest when his words are abruptly cut off.

"What's wrong?" I question when his face consists

of pure rage.

"We need to go right now. Sorry. I'll show you around another time, but I have to speak with my father. Come on, I'll drop you off at the house."

Confused I follow him upstairs and out of the building as we speedwalk toward the house.

Once inside Shepherd points in the direction of the hallway and says, "First door on the left is one of the bigger guest rooms. It's yours if you want a private bathroom, otherwise, a smaller one is right next to it."

"Private bathroom sounds great." I give him a small smile. "You go do what you need to do and I'll check out the room. Oh, I will probably head into town for some shopping before I settle in for the night."

"Sounds good," he rumbles. "Hand me your phone. I'll program our numbers in there so if something is up you can reach out to either one of us."

I hand it over and he thumbs the screen. His own phone gives a notification. He doesn't reach for it but keeps thumbing my screen before handing it back to me.

"I texted myself, so I have your number as well. Enjoy your night off. Romer will be waiting for you in the stables bright and early tomorrow morning." He takes a step in the other direction I'm going in.

"Thanks again," I tell him. "Really appreciate the job and the roof above my head."

"All good." He waves a hand into the air without

looking back and jogs out of sight.

I decide to check out the room first. My jaw hits the floor when I take in the large king-size bed, lovely yellow curtains, and a rocking chair with a closet and desk on either side. I have my own bathroom with a freaking rain shower.

I'm beyond impressed and happy with the living accommodations and the job, along with the steady income of course. Strolling to the window, I open it to let the fresh air inside. My ex hated my need for fresh air and I in return felt suffocated, keeping all the windows locked day in and day out.

At least now I'm my own boss and I'm not letting anyone tell me what to do. The corner of my mouth twitches at the thought of Hixon, who is in fact my boss, and with me living under his roof I'm not exactly my own boss. Nevertheless, I won't have a man boss me around or take decisions from me.

I'm thirty-one-years-old and it's about time I live my life the way I want. No compromising, no working my ass off for others, no negativity, no nothing but my own choices. A huge weight has fallen off my shoulders by starting over. I might not have anyone else to depend on, but at the same time, it feels liberating.

My parents would definitely freak out and be on the first plane back to the US if they knew what happened this morning. It's also why I'm dead set to make it work on my own. The roof above my head and the new job give me a huge confidence boost, causing a smile to slide across my face.

I grab my keys from my pocket and head out to my truck. The box with everything I own isn't heavy and I quickly carry it to my room. The smile is still in place when I make a mental list of the things I need to buy and jump into my truck. I whistle along with the songs on the radio as I head into town.

Once at the store I quickly have my cart filled to the brim. I arrive at the ice cream section and debate buying some. I really shouldn't add all those calories, but I deserve a treat. Besides, I'm set to work my ass off starting tomorrow and could use a little extra motivation.

I'm buying some lemon-flavored goodness for sure. Chocolate, maybe. Cherry, yum. Ugh. I end up with three tubs of ice cream when I carry the bags to the truck. Earlier I offered to make breakfast for the boys and I didn't look at what was in the fridge so I bought everything I needed.

Things are definitely looking up for me. When my parents asked if I wanted to take over the ranch last year when they made plans to move back to Italy, I was resolute with my decision. I just quit my job as a vet in the city because my boyfriend–my cheating scum, and now ex-boyfriend–complained about living alongside one another.

Which was true and due to my job. The travel distance back and forth to work, the stress that came from my job, add the struggles we had in our relationship and you have a full package of changes that needed to be made. I thought if I gave up my career and freed up my time to think about what I wanted out of life, we could mend our issues and come out stronger.

I should have been more realistic and maybe I was wearing blinders and didn't see most of our struggles. For one my ex wanted kids the second we started out, but I've always held off due to my career. When I finally gave in it became clear after months of trying that we had issues because I couldn't get pregnant.

We decided to get tested and we quickly learned my ex definitely had working swimmers, but I was the problem. I have a condition that prevents sperm from passing through the cervix channel. Maybe that's the reason why my ex dumped me for a younger version whose womb he could fill.

Great. I was in a good mood, but reminding me of everything in my life that fails blows my happiness to shit as I park my truck next to the other two in front of the ranch. At least I get to work with animals again. I should have probably mentioned to them that I'm a vet, but I haven't practiced in over a year. With everything going on I'd rather muck out a stall than stand in an operating room in the city.

Hixon is sitting in a rocking chair on the porch and is talking to his two sons when I step out of the truck. When I grab one of the grocery bags I hear shuffling of feet before Shepherd takes the bag from my hands.

"You don't have to do that," I sputter.

"No worries," Romer quips. "We're all about helping. Besides, you mentioned making breakfast tomorrow, right? Which basically means I'll be eating some of the stuff in here."

I can't help but grin at the boyish look he's giving me. These two men were definitely raised right. Taking the two bags that are left, I kick the door shut and follow the two brothers into the house.

Hixon mutters something under his breath and it takes a heartbeat or two for me to process it. I'm already inside the house when my mind registers his words and they make me rewind my steps.

Facing the grumpy bastard I snap, "I do not. If anything, you raised those two boys to show respect and be courteous. Somehow, I'm baffled they are and you lack those things."

I barely manage to bite back the words, "It tells me you probably didn't raise them since you're an asshole," because I don't want to be fired before I so much as have a chance to work. I stick my nose into the air and mutter under my breath, "Asshole," as I stomp into the house.

It could very well be my imagination, but I swear I hear him chuckle. Shepherd and Romer come out of the kitchen with smiles and fresh drinks as they head back to the porch. I take my time to put the groceries away. When I'm done, I take the lemon-flavored ice cream along with a spoon and disappear into my room.

Time to dive into a new book and enjoy the rest of my evening. Though, when I softly close the door of my room I completely forget the book when Hixon's voice flows through the open window. I don't mean to eavesdrop, but it's hard to miss when their voices are reaching my ears loud and clear.

Sounds like my life isn't the only one filled with drama. I stare down at my ice cream and mutter to myself, "I should have bought some popcorn instead."

CHAPTER 03

HIXON

I went to bed in a foul mood, but waking up to the sound of someone shuffling around in the kitchen at five in the damn morning is enough to fully wake the asshole inside me. Since both my sons are never up before six, I know there could only be one other person in this house awake, aside from me apparently.

Dragging my tired ass into the bathroom, I quickly wash up and handle my business only to return to my room and get dressed. My brain immediately gets hit with the issue Shepherd discovered yesterday.

Three other barrels of whiskey are missing. One of those was over twenty-years-old and one my father was fucking proud of. Apart from the emotional loss, it's also a financial one. All of that shit shoved aside? Someone stole from us right under our noses. And it's not the first time either.

We had one barrel gone missing the day my father died. He fell down the steps when he went into the basement of the distillery. I heard his screams and alerted the boys as we all rushed to the building. When I rushed down those stairs to get to him, he had already passed.

How the hell he could fall down steps he's gone up and down a million damn times is beyond me. The added fact of the missing whiskey barrel gives us the indication there's more to it than my father simply having a deadly accident.

I shake my head to clear it of the horrid memory and my nose instantly gets hit with the delicious scent of freshly baked bread. Fuck. The whole house smells the way it used to do when my mother was still alive. I swallow down the emotions clogging my throat as I step into the kitchen.

The windows are open wide and the little woman is humming a song while roaming around the kitchen barefoot. Her skintight jeans are covered in smudged handprints and her black t-shirt has powdered marks as well.

Her ass is swaying and her whole appearance is making my cock harder than it's ever been and it throws me off-balance enough to bark, "What the fuck do you think you're doing?"

She gasps as she whirls around. One hand goes to the counter to steady her, the other covers her heart.

"Holy shit. You hold the power to scare the bejezus right out of its skin."

I blink a few times to process her sentence and she takes the time to recover.

Pointing at the oven she says, "I'm making crusty Italian parmesan bread."

"I know," I snap. "I could smell it the second I stepped out of my room even though you opened the windows. Why the fuck are you up this early?" Reminding me of family, of a damn fine woman filling my kitchen, my house, my fucking mind with the things I've longed of for decades, I mentally add.

"Sorry." She looks as if I let the damn lid of the cookie jar fall on her fingers. "I couldn't sleep and thought I might as well get an early start." Her eyes slide to the window. "Am I not allowed to open the windows?"

A deep sigh rips from me and I rub my tired eyes and mutter, "I don't mind the open window. My mother used to do the same thing. Share the scent of home as it mixes with the fresh breeze of a new day."

"That's a perfect way to describe it," she softly says. "I always love the sense of freedom, feeling the breeze enter the house while I hear the sounds of nature. All these walls surrounding us can be suffocating. My ex–" She clears her throat. "Never mind. Would you like some coffee? I can make some."

"I'll do it," I find myself grumbling. "You can check on the food. I'm pretty sure those boys will wake soon now that the house smells–"

"Like Grandma was just here," my oldest croaks from the doorway.

I turn to face him and snarl, "Go back to your room and put on some damn pants."

Shepherd glances down and he shoots a sheepish grin in Clover's direction. I narrow my eyes at her, but she's shaking her head at Shepherd and seems unphased as she reaches for the coffee pot. I manage to grab it before she can, though.

"I said I was going to do it myself," I grunt.

"Okay, grumpy," she snaps.

Closing my eyes for a heartbeat, I find myself admitting, "There's a lot going on you don't know about, and I don't like to have strangers in my home."

"The stolen barrels?" she blurts and I whip my head in her direction to see her eyes widen as she slams her hand over her mouth.

"Sorry," she mumbles through her fingers. Dropping her hand she adds, "I wasn't eavesdropping or anything, I swear. I opened the window before I went into town to get some groceries and you guys were talking on the porch when I went into my room."

Again, I find myself rubbing my eyes. They flash open when I feel her bump her hip against mine.

"Move. I've been up long enough without a sip of coffee and all you're doing is stalling to make it."

All I can do is take a step back and let her do her thing. I swear this is the first woman who doesn't back away from me or run in another direction, which normally is the case. I don't flirt and haven't felt the need to sink into warm, wet pussy since my ex ruined my point of view involving all things involving women.

I know not every woman is like my ex, but believe me, when you've been in the line of work I'm in? Yeah, you've seen enough of the world to keep the crazy at a safe distance. Again…it was a bad idea to let this little curvy one under my roof. Even if the crusty parmesan bread she's pulling out of the oven smells fucking divine.

"Are you going to install cameras?" she questions and I have to blink a few times.

"I asked the same thing yesterday," Shepherd says as he strolls back into the room, this time he's wearing flannel pajama pants and a shirt. "Wait. Does she know—"

"Her window was open yesterday and she overheard everything," I grumble and sink down onto one of the kitchen chairs.

Shepherd shrugs. "Good. At least she's aware and can keep an eye out."

"She'll be doing no such thing," I snarl.

Shepherd's eyes widen at my outburst. I can't explain why I jumped out of my skin, but the thought of finding her at the bottom of the stairs, just like I found my father, is making bile rise up in my damn throat.

Clover, on the other hand, doesn't seem phased when she simply places a mug of coffee in front of me and announces, "Someone is in need of caffeine."

Shepherd snickers and I'm about to snap at him again, but I hear Clover ask, "How about you, Shepherd? Would you like some milk?"

This time I'm the one snickering at the way she treats him like the kid he is.

The corner of my mouth twitches when I remark with a hint of laughter in my voice, "He would, but add a little coffee too, to mask the taste."

Clover giggles and I find myself staring at her carefree features as her head tips back and her eyes close with crinkles of laughter surrounding her eyes.

Romer breaks the spell she put me under when he says, "What smells so damn good?" as he enters the kitchen.

"Have a seat and I'll show you," Clover quips and my youngest rushes to the table to plunk down as if he's a six-year-old that's promised ice cream instead of dinner.

What is it with this woman? I admit, her charm, great baking by the scent of it, and her whole appearance are something else. Since she also overheard our discussion yesterday, I don't have to hold back when she's around.

"I'm going to head out and pick up a few things I need to install the extra security. I want you two to keep an eye on the perimeter. The back door of the stable looks as if someone has tried to get in and I want a steel plate installed to prevent a second attempt,"

I rumble. Without looking at the woman I tell her, "Stay with one of my kids at all times, Clover. No wandering around the ranch alone until we know who the fuck has been stealing and trying to either get more or vandalize our property. I'm not asking, but I'm telling you as you're your boss. Understood?"

She refills my coffee and snaps, "Sir, yes, sir."

I narrow my eyes at the woman and without a second thought I snarl, "Fair warning. You can say those three words when I order you to bend over so I can fill you up with my cock. But when you say them mockingly as you did just now? You'll still find yourself bent over, but my handprint will be burning the skin of your ass. Am I clear?"

"Holy shit," Shepherd grunts.

"Not the first thing I want to hear at the breakfast table," Romer mutters.

I slowly turn toward my grown-ass sons, who are boys at times but sure as fuck are adults and know how to use their cocks. Not to mention, I've overheard loads of their talks about hitting pussy when they have a rare night off.

Directing my attention to Romer I remark, "It wasn't the first, but the second thing you heard at the breakfast table."

"Okay, I'm going to take a shower and get ready to work. Y'all can bounce the dirty talk off one another or keep discussing things you should go to the authorities about," Clover states and throws the cloth into the sink she was using to wipe the counter.

"Authorities won't do shit around here," I snarl, anger getting the best of me.

"That's because Daxton Claude fills their pockets so they don't care about anything that goes on in this town," Shepherd says, disgust overtaking his normal soothing tone.

"You're shitting me," Clover says and drags the chair next to me away from the table to plunk down.

I turn to face her. "I thought you were going to take a shower."

She rolls her eyes. "Go munch on the bread I made you while I pull some more rumors from your kids' mouths."

"Not rumors," I mutter and start to eat the delicious bread she made. "Fuck, that's amazing."

"Thanks," she throws my way but dismisses me when she turns to Shepherd. "Who is this Daxton Claude and what does he do for a living besides bribing the law? Oh, is he the one stealing from you guys? You know, try to make it seem like you need protection, so you'll pay him? Do you pay him?"

"Motherfucker," I grunt.

While both Shepherd and Romer mutter, "Fuck," at the same time.

I pin my oldest with a stare. "He wouldn't have caved."

"He wouldn't have told you about it either," Shepherd fires back.

"If they started their harassment they could have

very well pushed him down those stairs." Romer's voice is a mere whisper, but it hits just as hard as the realization inside my head.

We live far enough from the city and have held our firm ground when it comes to Daxton Claude. Of course, my moving back here and indefinitely working the ranch has kept that fucker at bay as well. Seems somehow, he's tried to slip by me because Clover's suggestion sounds like a reasonable explanation.

I shoot from my chair and point at Shepherd. "Make sure she doesn't stray. I'll be back later today."

Reaching for the plate in the middle of the table, I snatch another slice of delicious bread and head for my truck. We're going to need eyes on every part of my property to nail Daxton if he's behind all of this. Evidence to prove he's behind it is the only way to deal with this fucker once and for all.

CHAPTER 04
Five days later

CLOVER

The one thing that keeps me moving forward is routine. Every day for the past five days I've been getting up before everyone else and starting breakfast. The weather has changed. It's the end of October and I'm pretty sure it's going to snow soon.

The chilly morning doesn't stop me from opening the windows. Taking a deep breath, I stare out into the darkness. It's still another two hours till sunrise but that doesn't stop me from enjoying my morning.

I blow over my steaming cup of coffee when I hear a door open from the hallway. There's no need to guess who is strolling into the kitchen because Hixon is always the first one up. His two sons will sleep for another hour, but most would still consider them early risers.

Placing my mug on the counter, I reach for the

cabinet to grab one for Hixon. My breath hitches when I feel a solid, warm wall at my back and a large hand appears before I have a chance to grab the mug I was eyeing. Is that his belt buckle grazing my ass or is his dick as hard as metal?

"Here you go," he rumbles beside my ear.

My heart jumps in my chest and did I imagine his voice to be husky? His closeness takes my breath away and I'm completely stunned into a frozen position for a few heartbeats. Such a stark contrast from how he's been acting since I got here.

I admit it's like he's getting used to having me around. Starting with a sexual innuendo the first morning I made breakfast. Threatening to spank my ass or fuck me for that matter. Then there's a feeling I have that his eyes are on me whenever he walks into the same room I'm in. But this? Having him brush against me?

A shiver runs through me and I clear my throat as I move away to fill the mug with fresh coffee. Keeping my hands busy is enough not to think of his weird action, but as I place the coffee and bread in front of him, my mouth gets the better of me.

"Either you woke up horny and decided I'm the nearest female up for grabs or you need something else than a quick fuck from me. Which is it?" Surprisingly my voice stays matter-of-fact.

His eyes go wide for a fragment of a second before they narrow.

The muscle in his jaw jumps before he grits, "I

need a reason to be at the restaurant tonight and I can't turn up alone."

I reach back and grab my mug from the counter and turn to face him again. "Explain to me why you're taking me to…I'm guessing dinner with you mentioning a restaurant. I don't like being led on or confronted with a surprise. My ex fucking a decade younger chick in my own bed kinda makes a woman like me suspicious, doubtful, and lacking trust for those who have a cock between their legs."

A deep sigh rips from him and he rubs his beard. "Nothing has happened these past few days and I need to know what Daxton is up to. Shepherd thought he might be triggered if he sees me out and about. Especially if I'm with a woman as if there's nothing to worry about."

I move toward the table and slowly sink down into the chair across from him. "And why would Daxton be triggered if he sees you with me?"

"Because the fucker has always wanted everything I have," Hixon snarls. "We went to the same school, so it started early by wearing the same boots, hat, and jacket. Then as we got older, he tried to steal my girlfriend…which he couldn't. My ex wanted the classy reputation she needed to be where she is now. Being with Daxton wouldn't get her a desk job at the White House."

"Your ex works at the White House?" I gasp.

Hixon shrugs but the corner of his mouth twitches when he blows me away with his next words. "I was one of the president's bodyguards once, took a bullet and was medically discharged due to me both being in the military reserves and Secret Service."

I lean back in my chair, my eyes inspecting the kitchen ceiling as I slowly mutter, "Woooooow. I didn't see that one coming." A thought strikes me and my sudden lurch forward makes the chair scrape over the floor when I ask, "Is that why you're all badass and making a stand against Daxton? Do you still have some connections and are going to try to bring him down? Oh, I am so in. Do I get to wear a weapon under my dress tonight? Should I wear a dress?"

A growl rumbles low in his throat. "You won't get involved. And no, there is no bringing him down. I just need to know if my suspicions are reasonable or blown out of proportion. When you suggested Daxton's involvement a few days ago some things fell into place. I just have to see his face, his reaction, then I'll handle things accordingly through the proper authorities. He might think he's invincible but that fucker doesn't own all the law enforcement agents around here."

"You think he might have pushed your father down those stairs," I muse.

Hixon chews his bread and swallows before he tells me, "My father always told me to leave Daxton be. That his upbringing was the reason for his actions. Whenever I questioned him about it, Dad would always say decisions weren't always the right ones but sometimes doing the right thing was respecting choices made by others." He shrugs. "Whatever the fuck he meant by that. My father was a private person and it's the reason why he bought this ranch decades ago. He wanted a secluded place to live with my mother far enough away from people like Daxton and his father. He basically avoided people and only worked with a handful to sell the whiskey and horses we bred. Every time the name Daxton Claude popped up, he switched topics."

"And now it strikes you as odd." I nod, understanding his reasoning because it doesn't make sense and I admit, "It would nag me too. So…I'm in. Tell me what you need me to do, and I'll help."

He gets to his feet and takes his plate to rinse it under the tap. "Let's go for a ride."

My head rears back. "The surprises keep coming. Isn't it too dark out?"

There's a low chuckle. "We'll take care of the horses first and by the time we've saddled up we can catch the sunrise."

"Fine," I huff, trying to make it sound like I hate it but inside me utter joy is coursing through my veins.

I love taking care of the horses and riding for that matter. I've spent time with both Shepherd as well as Romer, but Hixon has kept his distance, even if we've shared the same space. I'm beginning to think his grumpiness is some kind of defense system and the man is finally thawing his icy attitude and is starting to warm up to me. One can only hope, right?

We walk into the darkness but the light above the stables guides our way. Hixon opens the door for me and hits the lights. The horses start to nicker and the smile I feel sliding across my face is one I'm sporting a lot these days.

Like every morning, I grab the things I need to groom and open the first stall on my left. I start with a vigorous rubdown and then switch from a rubber curry to a body brush. I'm combing the horse's mane when I hear Hixon close the stall across from me and then move to the one next to it.

I guess he's used to the routine and a lot quicker than me. Though, I don't see the need to rush because this makes me happy. Working with these magnificent animals is a gift, especially when the horse nudges her velvety nose along my cheek. A giggle flows from me when she snorts and blows warm air along my face.

"Okay, sweetie, you're done," I muse and pat her neck before I step out and lock her in.

"Did you always work at your parents' ranch?" I hear Hixon rumble.

I keep my back to him and start to groom another one of his mares. "Only when I visited them. My ex worked at their ranch full-time. I used to be a vet until I quit my job because my ex complained that I was never home." I release a deep breath. "That cuts the story a bit too short but it's basically the main reason I quit. He was right and I didn't like the workaholic I turned into. Though, it might not have created the best circumstances for our relationship either. I guess…neither one was happy with one another. My parents leaving the country, him losing his job. Circumstances," I muse, spilling my guts to the mare's stomach instead of in Hixon's face.

I jump a little when I hear his voice coming from right behind me. "You're a vet? Why wouldn't you mention something so crucial during the interview?"

Turning to face him I run my fingers over the brush I'm holding. "It would have made me over-qualified and might have made you question my motives. Besides, you weren't open to giving me the job from the start, so it wasn't really a normal job interview. I'm happy here, though. It's given me the fresh start I needed to leave everything behind me. Your boys have been amazingly sweet and kind to patiently explain everything."

I bite my lip to prevent spilling the words, "Unlike you," since he's here now and is acting somewhat civil. One never knows what goes on inside another person's head. Who am I to judge him for his grumpiness? It's his ranch, his home I've forced my way in…even if he grudgingly hired me.

My eyes find his and it takes a few beats of my heart before he gives me a tight nod. "Let's saddle up."

The first day Romer told me I could ride the black and white Gypsy Cob mare Roisin whenever I wanted. I've repeated her name a few times out loud to make sure I pronounced it right. She's an eight-year-old, born and bred on this ranch.

"Hey, Ro-Sheen," I murmur, overly pronouncing her name.

She nickers and turns in her stall to face me. I still can't believe this is part of my job. Where my days used to be filled with back-to-back surgeries, then being flipped to staying home more and helping out at my parents' ranch, to my life being completely turned upside-down by my parents leaving and my cheating boyfriend.

All crucial things that made me feel like a ball in the pinball machine life really is until I arrived here. Living at this ranch, caring for the horses, making breakfast, doing things around the house...all of it is what I can see myself happily doing for years on end.

I'm finally done getting Roisin ready when I notice Hixon leaning against the stall while holding the reins of his horse, Witness. The horse is magnificent but the man next to it? Ugh. Why does my boss have to be a ruggedly sexy older man?

His Stetson is drawn low, and I can't see his eyes but the grayish beard, strong forearms, defined biceps, and hard muscles tucked away underneath the gray tank he's wearing–while it's chilly this early morning in October–is definitely a mouthwatering visual.

Not to mention, the man wears his jeans as if they

are solely made to complement his ass. Yes, I'm crushing on my boss while the man has been nothing but grumpy toward me in return. Whatever, a girl can dream, right?

Besides, I know for a fact he's almost fourteen years older than me. I know I shouldn't have searched for silver fox romance books when I found out about the age gap between us. Now all I can do is let my mind wonder how it might be to have sex with an older man. One who doesn't trade me in for a young flower. Yikes. That sounds weird and I don't consider myself a young flower either.

"Are we gonna ride or are you going to stare at me some more?" Hixon's rumbling voice instantly brings heat to my cheeks.

In defense I grumble, "Here I thought you were the one staring at me, so I thought to give you a minute to shamelessly get an eyeful while I returned the favor."

Why can't I keep my mouth shut at times like this? And why does this man make me feel like an awkward teenager who has a crush on the popular guy in class? His rumbling chuckle is annoying as I stomp past him out of the stable.

CHAPTER 05

HIXON

The view of the pastures I've seen all my life has gained an extra dimension. Added beauty, depth–with her vision on life she isn't afraid to share–along with a few other bullet points I won't name. She's throwing me off-balance while I have a load of stuff on my plate to concentrate on.

Within this moment, I'm throwing caution to the wind and choose to stare at her profile as she rides one of my horses. The smile on her face is genuine and everyone who sees it knows the woman is in her element. Such a stark contrast to my ex-wife. She would wrinkle her nose at the thought of this ranch and wouldn't go near it.

"What's the reason for you glaring at me? I haven't said or done anything to annoy you…yet," Clover huffs.

Fuck. Even her name, Clover…find your own four-leaf green thing ready to be plucked to add to your luck. That's what she represents for me. Too damn young, too tempting, too beautiful, too fucking good to be true because due to my ex-wife I know how vile women can be.

I rip my gaze away from her and confess, "I hate women. My ex-wife is a bitch."

"Sorry. If it helps to know my ex is a bitch too. People really suck. I'm also pretty sure mine dumped me because I can't get pregnant. Maybe it was the pile of circumstances but…yeah…people suck." She releases a deep sigh. "At least you have two great sons who are amazing. They don't hate women… well, they don't hate me. It shows her being a bitch didn't taint them. They are sweet boys."

"Sweet boys." I snicker. "They might be adults and could kill with their bare hands, but they're still boys. I'm glad you see that, even if you're their age."

She makes an unfeminine sound. "Their age? Hardly. Did you not hear me mention my ex dumping me for a young flower? I've been taken out like yesterday's trash." She winces. "Not really. I practically ran out of the house myself with the need to bleach my eyes from seeing him fucking that young chick. Whatever. All I'm saying is…my ego took a hit. With my medical condition it doesn't exactly make me the perfect girlfriend material either." She stares off at the pasture on her right. "Not that I'm looking for a new relationship. If all of it taught me anything, especially these last few days, is the fact that only one thing matters."

"Which is?" I find myself asking.

Her eyes land on mine. "My own happiness."

The corner of my mouth twitches. "Smart woman."

"Not that smart because I can't figure out how to have sex without dealing with a man." Her eyes briefly hit mine. "Don't start about dating a woman. Love is love and all that, but I do like one part of a man. More than one part if you count a skilled mouth and fingers but–" A frustrating growl rips from her. "You know what I mean. I don't trust men enough to have a one-night stand, add the fact I don't have a private house…and why am I spilling my guts to my boss…who in fact hates my said guts."

My head tips back and a bark of laughter rips from me. "I don't hate your guts, peanut. I'm just annoyed by any woman, especially when they breach my space."

I bring my horse to a stop and wait for her to do the exact same thing, making the mare come to a halt next to mine when I tell her, "I wasn't going to suggest for you to date a woman. I might have told you to get a vibrator, but just the thought of you playing with yourself under my roof gives me visuals I don't need inside my head." I shamelessly adjust myself and her eyes go wide with understanding. "We could come to an agreement. One where we fuck without mixing business between us."

She swallows hard and croaks, "And how would you suggest we do that?"

"My cock filling your pussy, your mouth, maybe your ass if you'd let me," I deadpan.

Her eyes narrow. "The without mixing business part."

"We keep it inside the bedroom. No feelings involved. My kids can't know either or anyone else for that matter. The moment we get out of bed we're hands off, in the bed hands on."

"Bootie-call." She nods to herself. "That might work. But I do have one demand, though."

Now I'm the one narrowing my eyes. "And that would be?"

"Call me a tiny round nut again and I'll shove one through the slit of your cock and see how you like it," she growls.

I choke on my own saliva, but she doesn't notice 'cause she spurs her horse on and leaves me coughing up a fit. Clearing my throat as I catch up to her, she points at the small cabin at the edge of my property.

Completely jumping over what we just discussed she asks, "Who lives there?"

"Security," I grunt.

She brings her horse to a stop. "How come I haven't met or seen any other people except for you and your sons?"

I place my forearm on the horn of my western saddle. "They're doing their job right if they stay off the radar. I also only hired them a few days ago."

"When you installed the security system?" she questions.

Giving her a sharp nod, I feel the need to expand. "I hired two of my former colleagues who just retired. They were looking for a new challenge and I offered them the cabin, along with a nice paycheck to keep this place secure. It allows us to focus on the horses and the whiskey. Besides, I can install a security system, but if no one can keep an eye on it… what use will it do other than have the fucker on tape if they fuck up? I want to catch them in the act."

"Do I need to bring them breakfast?" she questions.

"Fuck no," I snap. "I don't pay them to eat, they can arrange for their own damn meals."

She tilts her head. "You're not just an ass to me, but you are one to everyone, huh? Somehow that makes me feel better." Clover jabs her hand through the air and leans in to offer it to me. "You have a deal. Sex and nothing else. But I do want it with a challenge without you being an asshole."

I take her hand in mine because I'd be an idiot to pass it up; it's been way too long since I shoved my cock in warm, willing pussy.

"A challenge?" I try to clarify.

"Spank my ass, grab my wrists, fist my hair, all that raw and hot stuff. My ex was a missionary type of guy with a three-minute limit of excitement once a week. I really wonder if sex is overrated or just blown out of proportion by romance books. So. Are you up for a challenge, old man? Because I want orgasms."

"Old man?" I grumble. "Sounds to me like your ex was the old man, but I'll make your pussy weep very soon, Clover. You'll be begging me to stop wringing orgasms from your body and even that won't stop me from pumping my cock deep inside you." I spur my horse on and mutter, "Three minutes, what a fucking joke."

I hear her whisper a soft, "Oh wow," and then we're enjoying the rest of the ride in silence. Once we return to the stable Romer is there to bring the horses into the pasture one by one and I leave Clover to help him.

There is a pile of work waiting for me in the office and I glare at the safe that holds the last will and testament of my father. He gave it to me a few months before he died and asked if I wanted to read it, but I didn't. I told him it was his last will so I was good with his decisions, whatever they may be. He told me he'd leave it all to me and as far as I know me and my boys are his only living relatives.

My phone starts to ring and I recognize the number. It's the lawyer and I really am not in the best of moods to handle it, haven't been since my father died. Not just died, but murdered. I'm fairly sure now. Why? I still have no clue, but my gut tells me Daxton is involved somehow.

I barely manage to get some business emails

handled, while completely ignoring my incoming messages, when Shepherd steps into my office.

"You could at least knock," I grumble. "There was no way you'd risk stepping inside if your grandfather was still sitting in this chair."

A sad look slides across his face. "He was slowly passing the business on to you and you're the one who always said the door was always open for us."

The corner of my mouth twitches. The man isn't lying. His mother might be a closed book and completely ignores the fact that she has two sons, but I sure as fuck don't. I made sure they know that as long as I'm walking this fucked-up world, I'll be there for them no matter what.

"Tell me why you're here?" I ask and close down the laptop sitting in front of me.

He jerks his thumb over his shoulder. "Didn't you make arrangements to go to the restaurant and check out Daxton? Taunt the fucker with your presence?"

I check the time and release a string of curses.

"Thought so." Shepherd chuckles.

Rising from my chair I pin my oldest with my gaze. "Listen. I'm going to take Clover with me to draw attention to me."

I lied to Clover when I told her my kid suggested I take her with me.

His eyebrows shoot for the ceiling. "Why would you drag her into something we don't know what the fuck it is in the first place? If Daxton is involved it's a huge risk, you know that."

"She's already involved if she works here," I counter.

Shepherd glares at me. "If you do this, he will take the bait."

My fingers curl into fists. I know damn well what he means because I don't have any secrets from my sons. They both joined the military with my permission when they were seventeen. Each of them went through special training and can get any job they want, have been hired as skilled SWAT members, but they both choose to work here at the farm. They have a lot of accomplishments for being pretty young, but it's just the way it is.

"Like I said, she's a target living in our home. This is not on me, but on you two," I grit. "The reasons why we needed to hire someone, and put the word out, was under strict restrictions."

Shepherd shrugs. "Coy texted his approval and I acted accordingly."

Coy is our government contact and why he would interfere with us hiring someone is beyond me. Not to mention, how the fuck did he know about someone showing up to apply for the job?

"What?" I snap. "Why are you telling me this now?"

The idiot shrugs again. "Instructions. The reason why I'm telling you now is that I know for a fact you'll answer his call. He's been trying to get a hold of you and you're ignoring him."

I grind my teeth. "I'm fucking working."

"Call him and I'll let your date know you'll be ready within half an hour." Shepherd doesn't wait for a reply but stalks out of my office without a second glance.

Releasing a deep sigh, I take my phone and make the call. Coy wants frequent updates, but when there's nothing to tell the man there's no reason for us to talk. Hence the reason I ignored his calls. Him ordering Shepherd to hire the one applying for the job the day Clover arrived here, though? Out of fucking line and I gave him an earful to let him fucking know.

Stalking out of my office, I quickly dash into my room to wash up and get ready to head out. Clover is waiting in one of the rocking chairs on the front porch when I step outside. There's a gleam of excitement in her eyes and I wonder if it's due to the prospect of sex or food.

Probably the latter. My cock is hard and I should feel shitty dragging her into this, but I'm done caring. For one I deserve something nice. Secondly? Bringing her along would challenge the fucker I'm trying to bring down. Adding a little heat is always a good thing. Business or pleasure, and for me it concerns both.

A Clyden's Ranch Wiseguys novella

CHAPTER 06

CLOVER

I would consider the booth in the far corner of the restaurant where we're currently sitting in romantic if it wasn't for Hixon ignoring me. His gaze and attention have been anywhere except directed at me.

Though, the waitress who came to take our order and who brought our drinks didn't get his gaze either. It's as if the man is a hunter who is completely focused on taking out his prey, whenever the prey decides to show up that is.

When we agreed to the deal to have sex I thought we'd be civil to one another. Hell, the horse ride this morning was somewhat normal 'cause the man clearly has a slice of grumpy to his mood any time of day. But ignoring me completely after asking if I could join him at this restaurant for dinner? Yeah, the assholery rises above and beyond in this man.

There's a small amount of wine left in my glass and I knock it back before placing the glass back on the table and raise my voice a bit when I ask, "Will I be getting your cock tonight the same way we have dinner? If so, I'm only agreeing to ride you reverse cowgirl style so I can return the favor by completely ignoring you."

The corner of his mouth twitches and the annoying man rumbles without sparing me a glance, "You won't be hearing me complain if you do."

The waitress arrives with our food and I lean back to give her enough space to place the mouthwatering dish in front of me. Wow. This looks amazing. I love being in the kitchen, baking or cooking, but this pizza looks and smells divine.

Hixon's pizza also looks tasty, but I don't think he'll allow me to reach across the table and steal a slice from him. My wine glass is filled when the waitress disappears again. I take a bite from my pizza and moan when the different flavors hit my tongue.

"I'm working. Your moans are distracting," Hixon announces.

"Then feel free to shove the ends of your napkin in your ears," I snap in return. "If I'm liking something I always enjoy it to the fullest."

"Noted," he grunts.

I narrow my eyes. "What?"

Hixon slowly chews the bite of the pizza he just took while keeping his gaze to something over my shoulder.

He swallows and when I take some food in my mouth he announces, "I'll stash your panties in your mouth when you take my cock later. If you're moaning this loud with food, I'm guessing you'll be loud when I fuck you and scream when you come."

A piece of pizza almost goes down my windpipe and I barely catch it with a cough. This time his eyes meet mine and there's mischief dancing in his blue eyes. How he can flip this switch from grumpy, uncaring to teasing, and genuine is beyond me.

I'm about to call him out on it when his whole face changes and a menacing glare hardens his gaze.

In a low voice he tells me, "Don't say anything and follow my lead."

My head rears back a bit and I frown as I process his words. My time runs out to wonder about his reaction when a man appears on my right. Staring down at me with his blue eyes and what I can tell is dyed black hair. There's no way it's his own hair color. It might have been once but the lines around his eyes and the rest of his face tells me this man is around Hixon's age.

"Aren't you a gorgeous one," the man murmurs and his eyes stay on me when he adds, "Hixon, where have you been hiding this beauty?"

I have to slowly draw air into my lungs through my nose to keep from replying.

Hixon doesn't have this issue and merely grunts, "In my bed."

I duck my head to hide the smile I'm sporting

and grab my glass of wine.

The sound of a chair scraping catches my attention and I glance up in time to see the man with the blue eyes sit down next to me.

"Daxton Claude. And you are?" he rumbles and holds out his hand.

My lips stay sealed, but Hixon is the one who's grunting, "Nunya, now leave us be."

"None of my business, eh?" Daxton laughs but it's without humor and to be honest? It makes my skin crawl.

"Now, now, Hixon. No need to be defensive. We both know this woman is too young and too good for you, aren't you, Clover Sterling?"

My eyes widen with surprise. How does Daxton know my name? Why did he introduce himself and ask repeatedly who I am while he knew all along? Hixon, though, doesn't seem surprised at all. The two seem to be in a staring match while I'm the subject of discussion.

"Mind your own damn business," Hixon snaps. "Now fuck off and let us enjoy the rest of our meal before I take my woman home."

"Mind my own business?" Daxton sneers. "Fucking hypocrite. How can you despise and judge my family business but sit here and enjoy a nice dinner with this princess here?"

Princess? Why would he refer to me as princess? Something only my father and brother would call me. I bounce my gaze between the two men and suddenly hate sitting here and am anything but hungry. Did Hixon bring me here as some form of statement? To taunt this man to draw out a reaction? He said as much, didn't he? But is there more to it than that?

Hixon casually reaches for his glass of water and takes a sip. His eyes find mine and the look in his eyes changes. It's as if he pushes away everything around us and only sees me. A woman he enjoys having sexual banter with when no one's around and acts grumpy on every other turn.

"You're right. I am enjoying a nice dinner," Hixon states and shoots me a wink.

I raise my glass at his statement and feel the need to add, "We're going to enjoy what comes next even more."

Daxton abruptly stands and turns to me when he says, "You're making the wrong choice, but you'll find out soon enough." He directs his attention to Hixon when he says, "Sharing might have run in both our families once upon a time, especially when it involved a married woman. With this beauty warming your bed I'm willing to make it a tradition. Feel free to send her over when you're done with her."

Daxton's eyes roam around my body and I instantly feel dirty. What a freaking sleaze.

"What was that about?" I whisper hiss when the creep is far enough away.

"I'm not sure," Hixon murmurs.

We glance at Daxton who is on the other side of the restaurant and snaps his fingers–making two people jump up who were sitting at the table he was occupying earlier–before stomping out the door.

"He gives me the creeps," I mutter and down the last of my wine.

The pizza I was eating before Daxton joined us isn't looking all that appealing right now, but I shove a piece into my mouth anyway. We finish the rest of our meal in silence and I decline dessert.

"I'm ready to head home if you don't mind," I tell Hixon and he nods in agreement.

The ride to the ranch is yet another long moment in silence, but neither of us seem to mind. We're both locked inside our minds, but I don't think it's for the same reasons. Hixon clearly wanted a confrontation with Daxton and I have no clue why or if he got what he wanted. I, on the other hand, am aware of my own skin.

There's a tingle low in my belly and I'm amping myself up at the possibility of having sex. It's been way too long for me and I've only had one sexual partner. I shouldn't hype it up inside my head, but I can't help it. Hixon has become a wild fantasy inside my head and I'm seriously hoping he'll break the mold I mentally made.

Said mold and the breaking is put on hold when Shepherd is waiting for us in the hallway when we step inside the house.

Shepherd points in the direction of Hixon's office. "A word, please."

Hixon doesn't even give me a backward glance

or excuse himself for that matter but disappears into the hallway. Anger hits me from being dismissed. I know we didn't exactly make it a fuck-date, but I thought with the whole flirting and insinuation we would have sex when we got home.

"Whatever," I grumble and head for my room.

I flip the lock and start my evening routine. Once I've showered and changed into an oversized shirt I dive into bed with a good book. About an hour later there's a soft knock on the door. Without looking I shove my middle finger into the air and keep reading.

Screw him. I know he doesn't see me flipping him off but let him think I'm sleeping, I don't fucking care. There's a lot I can handle but my brain is capable of cramping sometimes and it's PMSing when his personality is like a freaking pinball machine.

The book I'm reading gives me comfort and allows me to swoon into a world where men aren't afraid to let a woman know they are attracted to them. The whole touch her and die, fuck her good, and keep her pregnant and barefoot forever vibe.

Fiction is a pink, bubbly dream and reality is popping that bubbly shit because I will never find it in real life, nor will I get pregnant. To be honest? I've come to terms with that last little fact, but the fuck her good, touch her and die part? I'm still hoping.

I should probably get a dog to get the touch her and die vibe. A huge one with sharp teeth. Maybe I can teach him or her to bite Hixon in the ass. The corners of my mouth tip up and I feel myself grinning at the thought.

"What are you thinking about?" The rumble of Hixon's voice has me jolting up in my bed, my book flying into the air as I scream like the freaked-out chick I am.

His laughter fills the room.

Asshole.

I glare and snap, "How did you get in here? Why are you here?"

He throws his Stetson on the desk near the wall and moves to unbutton his shirt. I don't mind the silence and with it the lack of answers to my questions. My mind is fully in the gutter when he puts his defined chest on display.

One of his forearms is covered with a black and red inked sleeve. I'm licking my lips when I focus on his rough and large hands that are now working his buckle. Sliding it free from the loops he throws the strip of leather onto the bed and quickly starts to unzip his jeans.

Wowza. A naked Hixon is a sight to behold and I'm documenting every delicious inch of this man into my brain for the sake of future masturbation. The hungry look in his eyes along with the jump of muscle in his forearm as he palms his hard cock–that's straining toward his navel with a slight curve–and slowly starts to tug the fleshy monster.

My heart is racing and my pussy is clenching in

anticipation. Grabbing the hem of my shirt, I jerk it over my head and let it flow down to the ground. Hixon places one knee on the bed and I'm about to spread my legs for him to give him the space to nestle in between.

The man however has other thoughts and a squeal rips from me when he snags me around the ankle and my body instantly becomes a ragdoll. That's how easily the man handles my body as if I weigh nothing.

I'm not complaining, though. Not. One. Freaking. Bit. When I'm on my hands and knees and the man's hot tongue is sliding through the lips of my pussy to lap at the essence leaking from me.

His rough, callused hands have my ass in a bruising grip and I'm shoving my head into the mattress to quiet the moans ripping from me. Everything suddenly stops and I throw a look over my shoulder to see Hixon stand and glance around. He stalks toward the closet and roams around, only to come back with one of my panties in his hand.

My eyes widen when he pinches my chin and rumbles, "Open up."

I instantly submit to his demand. He shoves the fabric into my mouth. "Good girl. Now you can give me the muted sounds I like to hear coming from you."

Stalking around me he takes his position once again and a muffled scream rips from me when the sound of flesh hitting flesh fills the room. Heat blooms on my ass cheek but the pain mixes with pleasure when a hot tongue spears my pussy.

Fucking hell, I'm ready to orgasm on the spot and the man has barely started. I guess some parts of bubbly dreams do come true.

CHAPTER 07

HIXON

Ripe as a freshly plucked strawberry and just as fucking juicy and red. Fuck. I'm harder than ever. Licking her sweet and tangy pussy is only the start of what's to come but I'm already teetering on the edge. I smack her ass again. Muffled groans reach my ears as she grinds her center against my face.

I shove two fingers inside her and she instantly clenches at the intrusion. So. Damn. Tight. I can't wait for my cock to slide inside and fill her to the brim. It's been way too long since I've fucked and this curvy woman has been driving me insane for days.

Daxton trying to steal her from me had a surge of protectiveness roaring through me. Yet, this woman completely dismissed him and only had eyes for me. She tried to keep me out of her room, but there was no way I could let her slip through my fingers.

Not when she gave back as dirty as I threw the sexual innuendos her way. I have no clue how long or if there even is something long-term between us but the here and now is what counts. There is no age gap between us, no distance, no words, no arguments, no fucking nothing but two people who crave one another to the point of drowning in lust.

I curl my fingers and rub the right spot when she starts to strangle my fingers. She's coming hard and fast, moaning around the panties I stuffed into her mouth, riding my fingers and letting them soak in her juices.

Gritting my teeth, I let her orgasm fade for a few heartbeats before removing my fingers. I palm my cock and nudge the tip against her slick, puffy pussy. The feel of something brushing my cock makes me glance down.

This damn woman. She's rubbing herself while sliding her fingers around my cock as well. A growl rips from me and I reach for my belt. I wrap the leather around one wrist and grab the other to secure both of them behind her back.

"I'm in charge," I growl. "You take what I give, not the other way around."

I slide a hand up her back and tighten my fingers around her neck.

Leaning in I tell her, "I'm clean and you told me pregnancy isn't an issue, so if you're clean we're fucking bare."

"I'm clean," she croaks and it's all I need to slam forward.

Home. Balls-fucking-deep in tight pussy. My eyes cross and for a heartbeat or two, I keep the curvy woman pinned in place with one hand around her neck and the other on her bound wrists. She squeezes her walls around me and it rips a growl from my chest.

Her muffled pleads are challenging me and suddenly I'm up to proving to this little spitfire who is in charge. Sliding out, I slam forward and throw it on repeat. Skin slaps skin, sweat starts to form on both our bodies as I fuck her as if my life depends on it.

Hard. Rough. Raw. It's a burning need to make sure she'll remember who tunneled in and out of her body. Who owns her, ruined her for all other cocks. The soft pleads spilling from her body and the way she's rippling around my length is a warning that she's about to come.

She becomes even slicker and I keep her cheek pressed to the mattress as I let her wrists go to grab her ass cheek. My thumb grazes over her tight little hole and she clenches in warning to keep me out.

Not. Happening.

I gather some of her slickness and keep pounding her pussy as I rim her ass and shove right in. She locks tight before she unleashes and fucking hell she explodes like fireworks. Lighting right up and exploding into a captivating sight of beauty.

She strangles my cock in rapid waves and I grit

my teeth to hold back my own orgasm. I'm not a rookie and am in full control of my body. Doesn't mean I'm immune to her delicious pussy.

Letting my cock slide right back out I grip her hips and flip her over. It might be a tad uncomfortable with her hands behind her back, but this won't last long. My mouth covers her pussy and I eat her out like a starved man.

When she's about to fall into a sea of bliss, I stop and jolt up to palm my cock and slide right back into her tight channel. With a death grip on her hips, I pound her into the mattress until I feel that delicious tingle in my balls.

Ready to blow I feel the cum start to rip from my cock, spilling into her body and that's when I pull out. Fisting my cock I aim and shoot my load over her belly, tits, mound, everywhere I can let the thick ropes of cum brand her.

"Yeeeaaahhhhmmmmmggghhh," I grunt and let my head fall back to close my eyes for a fragment of vulnerability.

I never let go. I don't date, don't fuck, don't love, don't do relationships, but within this moment I give this woman all of me. My chest is heaving, my lungs are burning, and my heart is racing as I stare down at the woman who ripped my normality to shreds and embedded herself under my skin.

My gaze slides to my artwork and I feel myself smile. With one finger I rub my cum into her skin, sliding down and shoving it right into her pussy.

Pumping my fingers in and out of her until she's balancing on the edge of another orgasm once again. This woman wants her greedy pussy filled just as much as I enjoy filling it.

Lazily I watch her body overcome with pleasure as she rides my fingers through her orgasm. She sinks into the mattress and she must be uncomfortable as hell with her wrists still bound on her back.

Rolling her to the side I remove my belt and climb off the bed. I gather my clothes and open the door to check the hallway. Finding it empty I leave the room without a second glance. Yeah, I know it's a dick move, but what else is there to do?

We had an agreement to have sex. We did. I gave her orgasms and fulfilled her demands. Hell, I went beyond that and left her boneless, well-sated, and unable to say another word. Besides, I don't know how long she'll be around so it's better for us to keep it plain and simple. No cuddling, no kissing, no feelings.

I close my bedroom door and lock it. Dumping my things on the chair in the corner, I wander into the bathroom and take a quick shower. Her scent is giving me a semi hard-on and it's not something I can act on or need when I only have a few hours of sleep left before I have to work.

When my head finally hits the pillow I expect to crash to sleep, but instead, I find myself wide awake. I barely manage to snag an hour or two of sleep when my alarm alerts me of the fact that's six in the morning.

"Fucking hell," I grumble and slam the sheets away from my body.

I scratch my belly and stumble in the direction of the bathroom to go through my routine. Fifteen minutes later I'm dressed and craving coffee. These past few weeks I've woken up to the scent of fresh coffee and baked goods but the house is empty and lacking everything that's Clover.

My mood already went to shit with Daxton fucking up dinner, the information Shepherd told me afterward, and having my mind blown along with the cum ripping from my body. I thought I could fuck and be done with the woman but her pussy is a gem in a street filled with gravel.

I rub my burning eyes and make a pot of fresh coffee. Shepherd strolls into the kitchen and finds me sipping my coffee as I lean against the counter. He frowns and glances around as if he's searching for something, shoving his nose in the damn air to sniff as if that explains anything.

"She must be still sleeping," I rumble and the fucker narrows his eyes at me.

"What did you do?" he snaps.

Snorting, I place my mug on the counter. "Why would it be something I did?"

"Sorry," Clover mutters as she dashes into the kitchen and heads for the fridge. "I overslept."

She starts to pull things from the fridge and the cabinets and gets her hands busy making breakfast. Shepherd jerks his chin in her direction and I know he wants me to pop the question. A question we have both been wondering about ever since we received the information late last night.

I fill my mug with my second load of coffee when I casually ask, "Why didn't you tell us you're the sister of a notorious mafia boss in Rome? One who took over from his father and that's the reason why Daxton called you princess yesterday. As in mafia princess."

An egg slides through her fingers and lands in a splash between her feet. She releases a string of curses and snags some paper towels before she crouches down to clean the floor.

"Well?" I urge.

She throws a glare at me but quickly focuses on cleaning. "I have nothing to do with my brother and my father retired when we moved to the US."

"Why did they let you stay here by yourself?" Shepherd asks.

I cross my feet at the ankle and lean against the counter to sip my coffee, waiting for her to answer his question.

Her shoulders sag. "Because I didn't tell them I caught my ex cheating. If…if they find out I'm pretty sure I'd be on the next plane to Rome, but I want to live my own life. It's why my father retired early and bought the farm to give me my dream instead of being forced to marry someone I didn't know. No one in my family wanted to force the tradition upon me. My brother is eighteen years older than me and

I was kinda an oopsie baby. So, when I was ten my father let my brother take over and we moved to the US." She releases an unfeminine sound. "Funny how I ended up with a man I thought I knew and yet he too became a total stranger."

She wipes her hands against her thighs and her eyes find mine for the first time today. A faint blush slides across her cheeks and I like the way her eyes dilate. Clearly, she's thinking about every dirty little thing we did yesterday. I sure as fuck am.

"Sorry if my past…my family and background cause issues. I'll pack my things and leave." She hangs her head and takes one step forward.

"No issues," I find myself saying. Her eyes collide with mine once again. "Now get your ass moving to make breakfast so Shepherd here can stop whining about how I fucked things up. I'll be in my office." I step closer to Shepherd. "I don't want to be disturbed and be sure to bring Romer up to speed about what we found out yesterday."

"What did you find out? Is it about me?" Clover asks.

I don't spare her a glance but snap, "Your job is to make breakfast, Clover. Not sticking your nose into our business where it clearly doesn't belong."

I hear her gasp and Shepherd curses behind my back. I don't fucking care. There's more at stake than delicate feelings. This is a shitty world and if she's the mafia princess they say she is then she knows damn well how rotten life is.

CHAPTER 08

CLOVER

"There you go, love," I murmur and watch how Witness joins the other horses I also put in the pasture.

My boot finds the fence and I lean my forearm on it as well to stare at the beautiful creatures. The wind is chilly and the sky looks as if it's filled with snow. I love this weather. It was either Montana or Canada when my father retired so my brother could take over the business.

Our love for horses and snow is what drove us to move here and is also a part of the business according to my father. The last part is something I never asked about or was aware of. Yes, I'm not stupid and knew my family is the head of a large mafia empire, but they also keep the women safe and far away from that part of the business.

My parents wanted me far away from everything. Hell, I was a surprise baby and with my brother being almost eighteen years older than me the family didn't mind the shift in leadership. Especially since my brother agreed to an arranged marriage. Also, something my parents didn't want for me and why we moved here.

I take a shuddering breath and hope my time on this ranch isn't coming to an end. Last night was both a blessing and a curse. The best sex of my life and yet it wasn't intimate at all. We didn't kiss, no caring touches or anything close to it. Only carnal urges and lust sated with pure bliss.

My mind drifts back to the way he left me on the bed, covered with his cum and my panties still stuffed into my mouth. I should be thankful he at least untied me from his belt. The lacking closeness after those soul-deep orgasms left me feeling naked and it had nothing to do with the lack of clothes.

Hell, I still felt it when he ordered me to make breakfast this morning instead of providing an answer to my questions, making my place very clear. At least he didn't fire me right then and there now that he's aware I'm a mafia pr–

I gasp when things suddenly click inside my head. That's what Daxton meant when he told Hixon at the restaurant about despising his business while Hixon was having dinner with me. Daxton is mafia. That's why he knows who I am.

Shit. Which means Hixon despises the mafia

which isn't so surprising when you know the man has worked as a personal bodyguard for the freaking president. A good guy butting heads with a criminal, no wonder those two despise one another.

"Never gets old to watch for hours on end, eh?" Romer quips and I tear my gaze away from the horses grazing in the pasture.

I check my watch and realize I have been watching them for well over an hour while my mind rambled like a derailing freight train.

I give him a hint of a smile. "Animals are life no matter the size or breed but horses have always been my favorite."

"You used to be a veterinarian," he starts, but it's not hard to think where he's going with his thoughts.

"No, not horses, mostly dogs. I specialized in surgery to treat a torn cruciate ligament…knee surgery. It's a common surgery though the clinic I worked for specializes in certain procedures." I release a deep sigh. "I shouldn't have listened to my father when he arranged the job for me. To this day I still can't think of one reason why he wanted me to work in another state. Maybe he wanted me gone…build my own life away from them."

"Parents do weird things," Romer muses. "What's going on between you and my father?"

His sudden change of subject causes my skin to flush with heat, even if it's damn cold and snow is starting to fall.

"Nothing," I tell him and it takes effort to make

my voice plain. Taking a page from his book I switch the topic once more. "What's for dinner tonight?"

"I don't know." I can feel his stare on me.

Clearing my throat I ask, "Do we need to take the horses inside before the snow gets worse?"

"Probably," Romer mutters. "There's a snowstorm heading this way."

"Well, let's get them inside." I push away from the fence. "I'll head into town and make sure we have enough groceries."

"I'll go with you." Romer follows me and the snow is sticking to the ground by the time we have all the horses safely inside.

Romer points at his truck. "I'm driving. Did you make a list or do you have to check the house first?"

I pat the pocket of my jeans where my phone is. "Already have a list. Whenever I think of something or run out I add it to my notes."

"Smart," Romer mutters.

We hit the road and drive for about twenty minutes when I notice a man walking his dog.

I swirl my head in Romer's direction. "Do you think your father or anyone of you would mind if I got a dog?"

Romer winces and I guess I have my answer.

"No worries if not," I muse.

He parks the truck in the parking lot and turns to face me. "We had a dog named Bo. He was my grandfather's and I've known him half of my life 'cause he brought it home after he found it down the road from the ranch. The pup looked like it was thrown from a car or had fallen off one. They had to amputate one of his legs, but he was still hell on three legs. The horses loved that damn dog." Romer's eyes turn angry when he adds, "The day my father found him at the bottom of the stairs...later that day we couldn't find Bo anywhere. We searched for days but the day before you showed up, we found him in one of the pastures with a bullet in his head. They probably took out the dog before killing my grandfather."

I gasp. "Oh no. Who would do that?"

"No fucking clue," Romer murmurs. "Just like I have no clue if my pa would mind having another dog with something that will most likely remind him of what happened with Bo."

My throat clogs with emotions and I bob my head. "Thanks for explaining."

We exit the car and stroll into the grocery store. Pulling my phone from my pocket I check the list and put everything I need in the cart Romer is pushing. With the snowstorm and all, I add a few more items and an hour later we've loaded all the bags into the truck and are climbing back in and hit the road. I'm staring out of the window when Romer starts to curse.

"What's wrong?" I question.

Romer keeps his gaze in front of him and calmly states, "I'm fairly sure the brakes aren't working and a black truck has been following us since we left the store. They must have tampered with the brakes when we were inside the store."

"What?" I gasp and check over my shoulder. "What are we going to do?"

"I'm thinking," he growls. "Get Shepherd or my father on the phone."

My heart is racing and I take out my phone to hit Shepherd's number.

He picks up on the third ring and I ramble, "We just left the store and Romer says the brakes aren't working and we're being followed. The snow is fucking falling and the roads are slippery and I'm fairly sure we have a chance of crashing and maybe dying and I have no clue what to do."

"The fuck?" Shepherd snaps. "Clover, calm down and put the phone on speaker."

I pull the phone away from my ear with a shaky hand, hitting speaker as I glance at Romer.

"Sorry," I mutter. "I kinda freaked out for a moment, but I'm okay now."

"Good. 'Cause shit's about to become much worse before it hopefully gets better, okay?"

"Doesn't it always?" I deadpan.

Shepherd's voice fills the truck. "Dad's on his way."

"How does he know where we are?" I wonder out loud.

"Tracker," Romer mutters and I'm about to reply when there's a metal hitting metal sound.

My body lurches forward, but I'm held tightly by the seatbelt. It cuts into the skin of my shoulder. The car swerves across the road but Romer keeps it on track.

"Fucking hell." Romer throws a quick glance in the rearview mirror. "I had to hit the gas. All while the brakes aren't fucking working."

I keep quiet, not knowing what to say. To be honest, there's nothing I can say to help the situation. The truck behind us comes closer and I brace myself for the second hit. This time the truck seems to want to push us off the road.

I want to squeeze my eyes shut, but I can't. There's too much happening at the same time with the truck hitting us from behind–trying to make us crash–Romer trying to save us, Shepherd talking through the phone…and on top of it? The freaking snow that's making the road slippery.

"There's a gun in the glove compartment. If something happens to me and those fuckers try to… whatever. You grab that gun and fire, you hear me?" Romer's voice is steady yet rough.

"Okay," I croak.

His head swings my way for a heartbeat. "You do know how to use one, right?"

"Check if it's loaded, make sure the safety is off, point and shoot," I grumble, hoping my voice comes out believable. "It's been a few years since my brother made me practice."

The truck lurches forward when we get hit again

and this time we spin around. Without thinking I close my eyes when we spin and flip. The phone I was holding is thrown from my grip.

I have no clue if I scream or how long before it ends but the next thing I become aware of is a cold wind along with the ringing of my ears. I would say it's silent but somehow every sound is deafening and everything hurts.

Romer groans and I hear footsteps. My heart is racing and I try to move and feel my limbs. Something warm and wet is sliding down my face and I lift my fingers to wipe it away. I stare at the crimson on my hand and blink a few times to let the fact that I'm bleeding run through me.

Footsteps crunching in the snow make me aware someone is coming. I reach forward but the seatbelt keeps me in place. I mutter a curse and manage to free myself. The small handgun is in my hand when I quickly glance around.

My head is pounding and my hand is shaking. I suck in a cold breath when I realize we have come to a stop in a ditch when we flipped and crashed. The road must be on one side and a pasture on the other side of the truck but I have no clue which is which.

I do know there's someone on Romer's side. Black dress shoes come into my vision along with black slacks. My heart is racing and I remember Romer's words very vividly along with being hit and pushed off the road.

I have no doubt this person who is coming to

check on us this fast after we crashed is the cause of us sitting in this fucking ditch. I raise my arm and suck in a big gulp of air in the hope to steady my hand as I aim it past Romer and squeeze the trigger.

The owner of those black shoes falls back and scrambles away. I fire off another round and whimper when I hear the fucker return fire as it slams into the truck. My head throbs harder when I whip around to make sure the man doesn't catch me by surprise. I'm cold. Freezing. And all I want to do is close my eyes and sleep, but I can't.

"Romer," I whisper. "Romer, please wake up."

He groans but the sound of more gunfire causes my eyes to fill with tears. There are so many things I regret doing and more importantly not doing, but I guess it's too late now. If I do manage to live beyond this moment, I will make sure to live without regrets.

But I guess everyone wishes for a miracle when the darkest of moments of life throat punches you without warning.

A Clyden's Ranch Wiseguys novella

CHAPTER 09

HIXON

I'm standing in the stirrups and allowing Witness full freedom to run as fast as he can. In the distance, I see the flash of a gun and it causes an added rush of adrenaline to flow through my veins. I've been in many situations, but the one before me hits me square in the chest.

The impact feels greater than the bullet hitting me in the shoulder or the one in my leg I suffered when I was protecting the president. The first bullets fired seem to come from inside the truck and when I'm closer I can see someone running away, returning fucking fire.

I lean back and quickly bring Witness to a stop. The snow is a thick white blanket my boots instantly sink into when I jump off and start running. There's no way I'll risk my horse getting injured, but mostly?

I can move stealthily if I'm on two feet.

My first priority is to take out the fucker who is shooting at Clover and my son. Rounding the truck that's lodged in a ditch, I instantly spot a figure who is trying to get closer to the truck on the passenger side this time.

The fucker rounded the damn truck in an effort to take out Clover who I'm now sure was the one firing the gun. Darkness has fallen but the moonlight is giving me enough light to recognize the man who is trying to get Clover.

Pure rage hits me and I start to empty my clip as I stalk closer. Movement from inside the truck–the one that's still on the road and who caused the crash–drags my attention as soon as I've taken out the threat. No remorse fills me when I kill that person as well.

I rush toward the fuckers who were set to harm both Romer and Clover and make sure the threat is no longer there. The two people I took out were the only ones and I run toward the driver's side of the truck lodged in the ditch.

"Romer," I grunt and check for a pulse.

"Yeah," he croaks.

"He's been out for a few minutes, only groaning. His eyes stayed shut, but he did make some sound if I called his name," Clover rattles.

I reach for my phone and hit the first number on my list. "How far is the ambulance out? I need it now, dammit. Now."

Hanging up I let my gaze land on Clover.

"I'm fine," she mumbles and holds a handgun by the grip between her thumb and forefinger. "Can you take this, please?"

"Not yet," I snap and do a quick sweep of our surroundings. "Shepherd will be here soon along with some backup and an ambulance."

"Okay. My head hurts so if I do need to shoot and accidentally hit you or one of your kids I'm going to be really pissed."

The corner of my mouth twitches and I grunt. "10-4, wifey."

"I know I hit my head and all…but I'm fairly sure my name is Clover, not wifey."

Romer chokes out a laugh and I hear sirens coming closer. I have no clue why I gave her that nickname, but it damn well fits. Not only because she felt fucking good wrapped around my cock, but I've been enthralled with her from the moment I saw her. Even if I fought my attraction to her.

Moving around the truck, I get to Clover's side and carefully take her head into my hands. She has some cuts and lacerations, one of them above her eye and there's blood seeping down her cheek.

"Gonna need a few stitches," I murmur and check her pupils. "Headache?"

She slowly bobs her head and closes her eyes as she leans into my touch. Fuck. My chest tightens at the sight of her bloody face. This could be a hell of a lot worse. Fury flows through me and I grit my teeth in an effort to shut it down. Clover doesn't need my anger; she's endured my moody ass for days.

A dark SUV with flashing lights comes to a screeching stop and right behind it is a familiar truck. Shepherd jumps out of that one and the ambulance finally arrives to the scene as well. The sheriff hovers his hand near his hip where his gun is and carefully approaches.

"The fuckers that attacked them, who pushed my son's truck off the damn road, are dead," I state. "Now let those damn EMTs do their job."

"Hixon?" the sheriff barks. "Is that you?"

"Yes," I grit. "My woman and son need medical attention."

"I'm fine," Clover whispers and winces when she shifts in her seat.

The EMTs get to work and it allows me the time and space to stalk over to where Shepherd is standing. "I'm going to need you to follow the ambulance to the hospital and make sure those two are okay and bring them home if they are discharged."

"Done," Shepherd states. "What are you going to do?"

I jerk my thumb over my shoulder. "Bring Witness home and then I'm going to make a few calls."

Shepherd lifts his jaw in the direction of the crashed truck in the ditch. "Do you think Daxton caused this?"

"I don't think, I fucking know that asshole ordered the hit. Something is–" I don't get to finish my sentence when my phone starts to ring.

Taking it from my pocket I notice Sonny's name flash on the screen.

"What?" I bark into my phone.

"Ranch is under attack. Agents are on their way. Talk later." Sonny hangs up and I release a string of curses as I shove my phone back into my pocket.

"Gotta head back. Sonny said the ranch is under attack so I'm pretty damn sure this–" I point at the truck in the ditch. "Was a diversion."

I don't wait for Shepherd's reaction but jump into a run to head for Witness, knowing I'm faster if I go through the pastures rather than take the road by car. When I jump the fence I tell him, "Take care of them and call me later."

"Same goes for you," Shepherd bellows back. "Call to update me about the situation."

I wave my hand in the air as I grab the horn of the western saddle and jump on my horse's back. Witness has been my horse for years and knows exactly what I need. It's why she rides like hellfire all the way back to the ranch.

There are two of my security men, former colleagues of mine, waiting in front of the stables when I arrive. Three unmarked, black SUVs are parked in front of my house and I instantly know why they are here.

Gritting my teeth, I dismount and ignore those government fuckers and head straight to Sonny.

"When did they get here?" I grit.

"Five minutes before you did. Want me to take Witness and put her in her stall?" he questions.

I give a shake of my head. "No. I need the few minutes to take care of her to push my fucking anger down."

"Understood, boss," Sonny grunts.

I guide Witness into her stall and take a few minutes to take care of her while I try to clear my head. The sight of Clover and Romer trapped in that damn truck is still vivid in my brain. They could be in the fucking morgue right now if I didn't get there in time.

Making sure Witness is safely in her stall for the night didn't calm me down at all. If anything, I'm livid when I stomp in Sonny's direction. I notice Coy standing next to him and I should have known he would show up.

"What the hell happened while I was out saving my woman and son?" I snarl.

Coy slightly tilts his head. "Your woman? You mean Clover Sterling?"

I ignore the fucker and slide my gaze in Sonny's direction.

"We managed to capture one asshole of the two that were trying to steal whiskey barrels," he informs me.

"Show me," I grunt.

Sonny jerks his chin in Coy's direction. "They took him."

I whirl around to face Coy. "First you force me to take this case from your hands and now you're ripping it from me?"

"Till now I didn't realize things were this...personal." Coy shrugs. "Now I know it is and it might be best if we work together."

"Oh, you do, do you," I grit. "Well, then I'm done. Get the fuck off my land."

"Hixon, I don't think–" Coy starts.

"Fuck what you think," I snarl. "We're considered consultants for the government, but when I took this assignment I clearly told you I would see it through one way or the other. Including shooting him right between the eyes if I had no other choice. We have a signed contract that gives me the authority to do whatever I see fit. That fucker who was sent by Daxton to steal from me is mine to deal with."

Coy sighs. "You can have a go at him, but there's no need to force his hand. He requested a plea deal and started singing as soon as Sonny here put the cuffs on him."

I narrow my eyes, wondering what the fuck is going on. The time I had between rushing off to Clover and Romer and getting back here didn't take hours on end. Which makes me damn curious about what that thief had to say.

"What information, other than admitting he's sent by Daxton can he possibly have to get this deal from you?" I question.

Coy looks me dead in the eye when he says, "The man admits he entered your property to take a few barrels of whiskey. His boss told him it's his legal right due to a slice of his inheritance. He was told that if he ran into resistance he should let you know Daxton would go to court to get what's rightfully his. Basically? You need to pay the fucker to make him back off."

My phone rings in my pocket, preventing me from discussing this shit further with Coy. A good thing because my mind is still trying to process the damn details.

"I gotta take this," I snap when I see it's Shepherd calling me.

Stepping away from them I answer and Shepherd instantly says, "They are keeping Romer overnight. There are two uniforms in front of his room to keep watch. Good enough or should I stay?"

"Good enough. How's Clover?"

"Pissed. Cranky. Five stitches but otherwise she's okay." Shepherd chuckles. "She wants a bath and her own bed. There was also some talk about groceries being ruined and needing to go to the store again."

"Bring her home and make sure those fuckers in front of Romer's room don't leave." I glance back at my men and make a decision. "I'm sending Sonny over so tell them to expect one of our own to join them."

"Understood," Shepherd grunts and ends the call.

Strolling back, I face Coy. "I want a detailed report on the shit that fucker said. My boys and I will process everything and decide how to deal with this." I take a step closer and snap, "For future reference…I don't appreciate you bringing in other players to see how shit plays out. This isn't a fucking game, asshole. Clover doesn't deserve to be dragged into the middle of it. Especially when you knew she would draw Daxton's attention. I won't forget this shit."

Dismissing him I turn to Sonny. "Go to the hospital and protect Romer. They placed two uniforms in front of his room, but I don't trust any of them."

"On it, boss," Sonny grunts and jogs off to his car.

Without another word, I head for my office. Anger is still swirling hot through my veins. Last night after I returned from dinner with Clover, Shepherd explained how Coy interfered with Clover's life.

First letting Hay know I was looking to hire someone and then by making sure Shepherd knew we needed to hire her. Dammit. She could have easily lost her life all because Coy wanted to draw Daxton's interest.

Stupid fuck. Daxton's reasons were never clear, other than being a criminal who thinks it is normal to squeeze money from people. Mob boss or not, he's going down. If the fucker thinks he has any right or say on what belongs to me, he's dead wrong. And I'm going to show him exactly how I deal with him.

Soon.

Real. Fucking. Soon.

CHAPTER 10

CLOVER

I rub my eyes and instantly regret the move. Hissing through my teeth I drop my hands and push my upper body up from the mattress. My lungs fill with air and I slowly let it out through my nose.

Turning, I glance at the alarm clock on the bedside table and become aware it's a little after three in the morning. The events of yesterday come rushing back and I'm suddenly wide awake. It's a stark contrast compared to five hours ago when Shepherd drove us home from the hospital.

Hixon locked himself in his office and all I wanted was a hot bath and my bed and that's exactly what I did. Once my head hit the pillow after I soaked in the tub I completely crashed for hours. Until now.

I swing my legs off the bed and wander into the bathroom to take care of business. I'm wearing an oversized flannel button down shirt I use as a cozy nightgown and it comes to mid-thigh. No bra but I do wear panties and it's why I feel confident enough to step out of my room and tiptoe into the dark hallway.

The house is silent and I walk into the kitchen to grab a bottle of water from the refrigerator. Twisting the cap, I take a few big gulps and screw it back on. I feel the need for something stronger and notice the bottle of whiskey on the counter.

Shepherd has let me taste a few of their own whiskeys, but it's not for me. Though, I could use some now. I reach for the iPad on the kitchen table and quickly search for a recipe for a whiskey cocktail.

Some squeezed lemons, mint, syrup, crushed ice, whiskey, and fifteen minutes later I have a pitcher filled with whiskey cocktail that tastes divine after I've had my second glass. I don't even mind sitting here alone in the dark at the kitchen table.

It's kinda soothing, but I might as well take the pitcher back to my room so I can read a book. I step out of the kitchen and go back to my room. I glance down the hallway and notice some faint light coming from underneath the door of Hixon's office.

There's no sound and I wonder if he fell asleep in there. It's the middle of the night and I haven't seen him since he came to our rescue. Without thinking I find myself rapping my knuckles against the wood before grabbing the handle and stepping inside without waiting for a response.

Hixon is sitting in his chair behind his desk. In front of him are documents and an empty whiskey bottle with a glass sitting right next to it. His head slowly comes up and the look in his eyes causes an ache in my chest.

My feet move and I find myself standing close to him. Placing the pitcher on his desk, I let my fingers slide through his short grayish hair. He leans into my touch and closes his eyes as if he needs me to recharge.

"Daxton is my half-brother," he rambles and I suck in a sharp breath.

"What?" I whisper, unsure if I heard him correctly.

His gaze lands on mine and he grabs a handful of papers in front of him and raises his fist before letting them tumble down. "My father explained it from the fucking grave. He wanted me to find out sooner, but instead of telling me straight to my face he merely suggested to go into the safe and read his will. At the time I couldn't care less and told him so, demanded he enjoy everything he had in life instead of saving it to hand it over to me." He shakes his head. "He knew how much I hated those fuckers. Growing up in this place and watching them run this town with fear and extortion. Hell, it's why I went into law enforcement and eventually ended up in the White House."

I have no clue what to say to all of this and stay

quiet. Hixon jolts up from his chair and starts to pace.

"It's no wonder my father was the only one in town skipping the extortion. They left him alone because my mother's twin fooled him. They were carbon copies of one another and she lured her sister away one night to slip into her bed and let her brother-in-law fuck her so she'd fall pregnant. My mother caught her sister slipping out of her bedroom."

Hixon stomps over to the desk and hands me a handwritten note.

"Read it. Read how my father pours his emotions out on paper. How he's fucking crushed, humiliated, how he's confronted with his wife's hurt that he cheated on her without knowing. How her own blood betrayed her because she feared for her own life if she didn't fall pregnant," he snarls while I quickly scan the note.

The details I read and hear are devastating and I don't even have a part in any of it. I can only imagine how Hixon feels finding out like this, but it's heart-shattering for both his parents.

"I'm thinking my aunt didn't die in childbirth. That asshole knew Daxton wasn't his but he chose to keep his heir he finally got because the fucker was infertile." His eyes are blazing as he steps closer to me. "Now Daxton thinks he can come here and take what's mine. Take the ranch 'cause he's my father's son? Fuck, no. He fucking killed my father. My father."

I place the note on the desk. "Why is all of this happening now? I get the fact that your father wanted you to know and that it was a black spot in his life that festered. He wanted to keep it from you, but knew he can't…but why is Daxton doing this now? What changed? Why did he kill your father when this secret has been kept for decades?"

Hixon grits his teeth. "That infertile fucker who raised Daxton as his own died two months ago and I'm guessing he spilled his secret on his deathbed."

"Oh," I whisper. "That makes so much sense now. Holy shit what a mess."

"A mess that cost lives. And Coy willingly pulled you into it as well."

Coy? I frown and ask, "Coy? Who is Coy?"

A deep sigh rips from him and he rubs the back of his neck. "I never completely retired and take assignments as a consultant. My sons and I receive files on cases they either want our opinion about or take over and solve it for them. Once we've targeted a suspect and have gathered evidence, we bring in a team and either close the case ourselves or hand it over for them to end it. They've been asking us to take down Daxton because his father has become too big of a player in the mafia but he was grooming Daxton to take over. Needless to say, we finally took the assignment. Coy is our government contact and he asked Hay to tell you we were looking for help. He shoved you our way and into the path of Daxton."

I gasp and take a step back, my mind reeling with every single piece of information. "Do you think he knows about you and Daxton being related?"

"I don't fucking know if he knew before I did but they sure as fuck know now. The break-ins, my father's death, everything is linked to Daxton wanting what's mine and he's sent men with instructions to take what he thinks belongs to him. We caught one of his men and he's been a waterfall of information. Now I have to explain everything to my boys and I can't even wrap my own head around this shit," Hixon snarls.

I reach out to wrap my fingers around his muscled forearms. "Hey. None of this is your fault and by the sound of it, neither was it your mom or dad's. Even if your aunt felt as if she didn't have a choice, it still doesn't justify her actions. She should have reached out to her sister or brother-in-law in a completely different way. It's in the past, though. You guys will have to deal with it, but the guilt doesn't belong on your shoulders."

He stares down at me and the torment in his gaze is putting pressure on my chest.

"It's not your fault, even if the burden ended up on your plate," I softly tell him.

Hixon cups the side of my face and his thumb hovers over my eyebrow where the stitches are, due to the incident from last night.

"Your life should never have been put at risk," he murmurs. "You were unwillingly thrown into this mafia shit."

This little bit makes me snort. "I hate to remind you, but I was actually born into it. My parents wanted me out and look where that got me. A boyfriend who forced me to give up my dream to work with animals and threw me out after cheating on me. There are many ways and forms the people in my life have tried to protect me and yet life will always find a way to pull the rug from underneath your feet. So. Let me tell you something, Hixon. The sex you gave me was worth the risk. Even if what we had only lasted one night and you didn't even kiss me." I shrug. "Still better than wasting years with my ex in comparison."

His chest is rapidly rising and falling while his stare holds me captive. So much emotion is swirling in his gaze. I'm about to press the issue once again to remind him how none of this is his fault but I'm prevented from doing so when his mouth suddenly crashes over mine.

I moan into his mouth when his tongue swirls against mine. The taste of whiskey hits me and the feel of his hands firmly pulling me closer to him allows for tingles to spread throughout my body.

Sliding my fingers up, I dig into his shoulder and my other hand travels to the back of his neck. I'm relishing in the feel of this man being able to let everything around us fall away until there's nothing but the two of us.

The here and now where pleasure and lust are

brimming our bodies, clouding our minds with the urge to give each other what we desire–what we need–to move forward from here on out. And moving forward we do when he hoists me up, allowing me to wrap my legs around his waist as he places my ass on his desk.

It's a whirl of hands pulling at fabric as we frantically shed our clothes. I'm naked before him but Hixon only unbuckled his belt and shoved his jeans down his legs to grab hold of his thick cock to place it at my center.

He's leaning over me, our faces inches apart when he slowly fills me up to the brim. My pussy stretches to accommodate his thick length but it's a burn that causes sparks of fire to simmer through my veins. Fuck. This man is everything I ever wanted and more. Even his grumpy side is sexy but the fierce, possessive way he's staring down at me is breathtaking.

"Mine," he growls as he slams forward. "Mine to fuck." Thrust. "To take." Slide out. "To spoil." Slam forward. "To ravish." Each statement is stated in a steady rhythm as he warns me about the consequences involving both of us. "I'm not letting you walk out. They threw you in my path and I'm taking it. Taking all. This pussy. Your mouth. I'll be fucking your ass soon and I know it will be even tighter than this sweet pussy. And you're going to let me, aren't you?"

"Yes. Yes! Harder," I demand and with the next

slam inside me, he changes the angle making me scream, "Fuuuuck! Yes. Yes to all."

"Say it," he growls and wraps his huge hand around my throat. "Tell me who you belong to."

"Yours," I whimper as I feel the wave of my orgasm threatening to crash over me. "All yours, Hixon."

"Damn right you are," he grunts and fucks me into oblivion.

I scream out my release, but it's muffled due to his mouth crashing over mine. A devouring kiss that turns sloppy when he fills my pussy with his cum. My orgasm is sated by his seed as his cock twitches and pulses inside me.

This. This right here is bliss no other person on this planet has been able to give me. I don't care about the havoc, the history, the why, and the how. All I care for is this man and how good he makes me feel.

Life is all about making choices and I chose Hixon, even if he comes with a deadly form of baggage.

A Clyden's Ranch Wiseguys novella

CHAPTER 11

HIXON

My mind is clear and I've regained focus on the tasks at hand. All of it is due to the woman who is currently making breakfast as if all is fucking well. I was stuck with everything that was going on and in the dead of the night she simply swoops in, takes all the information I throw at her, and hands me back the clarity I need.

All due to her acceptance, letting me into her body, and taking me to bed to catch a few hours of sleep. I woke up with a determination to handle Daxton and it's all because of her. Where my ex-wife was filled with paranoia about the risks of my job, hated the ranch life, and loathed her own damn kids except for how pretty their pictures were displayed on her desk…all while Clover is the complete opposite.

She's selfless, strong, brave, thoughtful, caring,

and uplifting. Everything my ex wasn't and I can't believe I almost pushed Clover away due to personal experience and assumptions. Then the suggestion to only accept getting inside her pussy. Thank fuck I came to my senses before it was too late. There's no way I'm letting her go; not now, not ever. She's mine in every way and I made it very clear to her as well.

"I'll never get tired of this delicious scent," Shepherd states as he strolls into the kitchen. "Reminds me of Grams, of home…all while I am home. Fucking perfect."

Clover turns to grin at my son. "Have a seat, the bread will be done in three minutes. Hixon, mind getting him some coffee? I'd like some as well."

Shepherd's jaw practically hits the floor when I push away from the counter to do my woman's bidding. His eyes join his jaw when I lean in to brush a kiss on her temple first. He's still stunned when I place a mug with steaming coffee in front of him.

I help Clover place the food on the table and when we're all sitting down I tell Shepherd, "I called the hospital. Romer is coming home this afternoon. Sonny is still with him and can bring him unless you want to go."

Shepherd takes a sip of his coffee and assesses me. He's a smart kid, always has been and it's why he's also damn good at his job when it comes to reading people.

"Sonny can drive him since he's already there. I'm guessing Romer is out of the running for whatever you have planned for today. So. Why don't you fill me in and we'll go out and fucking do it already."

The corner of my mouth twitches. Like I said; he's fucking smart as a whip.

"Turns out, Daxton is my half-brother and I'm going to kill the fucker," I inform him with a steady voice.

Shepherd's jaw hits the floor for a second time and his gaze slides to Clover before landing back on mine. He's stunned into silence. I tear a piece of delicious cheese bread and pop it into my mouth.

Clover rises from her seat and grabs the pot. "More coffee anyone?"

Shepherd shakes his head. "Is this shit for real? What you just said?" He jerks his thumb in Clover's direction. "She's right here, you know. And why isn't she freaking the fuck out?"

Clover concentrates on filling her mug when she mumbles, "Because she hates Daxton's guts for everything he did and would rather see his life end than any one of yours. Not to mention, I remember very vividly how Romer and I were pushed off the road and were lying in a ditch when someone came at us with a gun. Now. Do you need more coffee or not?"

Shepherd chuckles and holds out his mug for her to fill while I start to explain everything I've learned about our family background. This time instead of dropping his jaw, he listens intently and leans back in his chair to process everything.

"I'm going to check on the horses," Clover announces after she's put the dishes away.

I take my phone and shoot the guard outside a text. "Lars will join you." She's about to slip past me when I snatch her wrist. "Aren't you forgetting something?"

She frowns and I give her wrist a little tug to pull her closer. She catches on with a slight chuckle and leans down to give me her mouth. I slide my fingers into her hair to keep her in place as I deepen the kiss and swirl my tongue along hers to taste her.

Pulling back, I smack her ass. "Now you can go."

She snorts and leaves the kitchen, allowing me to watch her curvy ass sway away from me.

"There's something I've never seen in all my life," Shepherd murmurs in awe.

I drag my attention away from the door Clover just disappeared through. "What?"

"You like her," Shepherd states. "You more than like her. Holy shit. I've never seen you act or so much as look at a woman the way you did just now. Not even our mother showed or received affection."

I wince at the guilt I feel rushing through me because he's right. At the time I thought I'd love my ex-wife, but I was wrong. I might have had feelings for her at the time, but I was young and ambitious. Blinded by the relationship my parents had and I wanted the same thing they had.

Except, I realize now that what they had was unique and founded on basic necessities.

A connection, mutual attraction, acceptance, trust, loyalty, understanding, and most of all respect. Knowing what went on between my aunt and parents shows how much they had overcome together and still remained loving partners till death parted them.

My ex was lacking in all departments but Clover is rising above it all. Till now I have been blind, but that woman is an eye-opener on so many levels.

"I do," I admit. "For me, she represents wildflowers blooming mid-winter. Exceptional beauty and a miraculous encounter. I'd be a fool to pass up something this rare. We both have a past and have scars that run deep when it comes to emotional baggage. Not to mention, our age difference for one but also the fact that she is younger and I already have kids." Shepherd glares at me and I add, "Adult ones. She can't get pregnant herself due to some medical issues—"

Shepherd holds up his hand to cut me off. "There are other ways like adoption. Then again, Romer might knock up a chick and give you two grandkids to fuss with."

I blink a few times and cringe. Shepherd chuckles, knowing it takes a lot to shock me but being a grandfather is definitely something I didn't think about till now.

"You know." Shepherd grins. "Romer did mention something to me when I was with him at the hospital."

"What?" I question, glad to skip over the grandpa part.

"She might have asked him if we were okay with her getting a dog." Shepherd snickers. "That's a good start."

I grimace at the reminder of our last dog, my father's dog, and the way I found him days after my father's death. Fuck, but I miss having a dog around the ranch.

"I'll think about it," I mutter. "First we need to take Daxton down and then we'll see if we can get that woman a damn dog." I get to my feet. "Let's head into my office and discuss our options."

Hours later we're changing into our gear and strapping on our bulletproof vests along with the necessary weapons. I've assembled a team and texted Coy we're going to hit Daxton's place as soon as night falls, which will be within half an hour.

"Should you be joining them?" Clover asks, her hands tightened to fists perched on her hips while she glares at Romer. "You're still recovering from a concussion."

He shoots her a grin. "Yes, Mom. I'll be fine," he teases, but I can see how my son appreciates the way she fusses over him.

"I'm not your momma," she huffs. "If I were, you'd be in bed and not gearing up to hit a mobster's house."

The boys and I chuckle and it does nothing to calm her nerves. Her jaw is set, eyes filled with anger and concern, and I do have to say, I wish she was my boys' mother. At least then they would have experienced motherly care. The thought sobers me up and I close the distance between us.

I pinch her chin between my thumb and forefinger to connect our gaze. "He will be fine. Romer is staying in the back of the SUV to oversee the mission. He'll be giving instructions when needed through our earpiece. Okay?"

Her shoulders somewhat relax and some of the worry slips from her gaze when she echoes, "Okay."

"Good," I grunt. "Same goes for you. Stay put so I don't have to worry about you."

Clover narrows her eyes and I feel the need to give her something to get her mind off the situation at hand.

I tip her head slightly back. "I should get you a dog to stay by your side at all times for an extra set of eyes."

Pure joy fills her face. "You should," she quickly agrees.

"We'll discuss it when we get back. For now, you can check the shelters if there's one we can adopt."

She pulls her face from my grip and reaches out to wrap her hand around the back of my neck to pull me down. I go willingly to take her lips in a scorching kiss, not giving a fuck that two of my men, along with my two sons, are in the room with us.

"Holy shit," I hear Romer mutter.

"Yep, he's a goner. They look good together,

though," Shepherd remarks.

"She's too good for that old fart. Let's hope she never finds out so she sticks around. I love her baking and cooking and hate to lose it. She's good with our horses as well," Romer fires back.

Pulling away from my woman I growl, "She's quite aware so shut the fuck up. Not that I'll give her a choice 'cause she agreed to be mine and I'm never letting her go."

"That goes both ways," Clover fiercely tells me. "Make sure you come home safe, and I'm holding you to your promise to get me a dog. If you come home injured and unable to come with me to the shelter, I'll pick two. A fluffy tiny one I can carry around, and a larger one who will bite you in the ass every time you turn."

I chuckle and shake my head at the things this woman manages to come up with. I gently squeeze the back of her neck and murmur, "Be back soon."

One last kiss and we're heading to the two SUVs we've loaded up. One holds extra weapons and other shit we might need, the other is equipped with laptops and screens so Romer can keep in contact with all of us and see what we see through the body cams.

We might not be an official SWAT team, but we have the special equipment, along with the authorization to act accordingly. Shepherd is wearing his Stetson and I shake my head. The fucker always goes against the grain with these things.

"Cut it out and wear the mask," I reprimand.

"Your Stetson is the color of the damn moon, making them spot you from miles away. Kinda defeats the purpose of wearing black."

He grabs his Stetson and takes it off just before taking a seat inside the SUV. I shake my head and get behind the wheel. We drive around town to get to Daxton's place. We've already gone over the blueprint of his house and know each and every room, door, exit, and whatever we need to know.

We rarely go in blind without knowing how to get out of a place. It's the difference between having an escape or getting trapped and in the end, can save your life. My phone rings when we park, and I curse myself when I see Coy's name flash the screen.

"I should have put the damn thing on silent already," I mutter as I answer the call. "What?"

"Change of plans. You need to detain him. We need him alive so we can force him to cooperate," Coy demands.

I shake my head in denial, knowing he can't see me. "Not happening. There's no way he will agree to be a rat. He's the damn head of the mafia family, asshole. Daxton will swallow his own tongue before giving you any kind of information."

"Find a fucking way. We just received information about Cerise Trenta, an Italian mob boss whom Daxton owes some kind of blood debt to. He's one of the main players the government wants to take out ever since the asshole set foot on US soil. Trenta is linked to a lot of shit, but we can't prove anything.

We need inside intel only Daxton's connection will give us, Hixon."

"No guarantees. I won't know until we get inside," I grunt.

Coy releases a sigh. "I'm texting you some information. Check it out before you go in. And Hixon?"

"What?" I snap.

"Find. A. Fucking. Way," he growls and hangs up.

I glare at my phone and scan through the images he texted me. I put it on silent before tucking it back into my pocket. Shepherd puts his mask on and we check our earpiece, making sure everything works before we split up and enter Daxton's property. I add a silencer and I nod at Shepherd who leads the other team as Sonny follows me.

"I've hacked into his system to turn off the alarm and placed his camera feed on a loop," Romer informs us through our earpiece.

A healthy dose of adrenaline floods my veins when I take aim and take out the first guard walking alongside the house. A soft pop beside me, coming from Sonny's gun, flows through the air as the second guard goes down.

"Perimeter is clear," Sonny states, knowing Daxton has two guards on the outside and three on the inside.

The fucker never married and didn't have any kids either. He's living in this mansion by himself since his father passed. We enter the fucker's home and I hear soft chuckling coming from a room to my left.

I signal over my shoulder to let Sonny know I'm taking lead while he has my back. The two guards sharing a drink are startled into action and both reach for their guns. I don't hesitate and a heartbeat later the both of them crumble to the ground, eyes as lifeless as their bodies.

Backing out of the room, I head for the office located at the end of the hallway. Light is coming from it and there's a murmur of voices that have me second-guessing if the man is alone. I glance over my shoulder and Sonny shrugs.

"Does the fucker have company?" I whisper into my earpiece.

"No," Romer instantly answers.

There's a hushed breath coming into my ear before I hear Shepherd state, "Looks like he's talking to different screens sitting on his desk."

Shepherd and a few of the others were going around back but I guess the fucker rushed out to glance through the window to get us the information we needed.

"Affirmative," I grunt. "Going in."

I swiftly enter the room and feel Sonny right next to me as we aim our guns at Daxton's head.

"Time to clock out, asshole," I snarl and within a few strides I have the barrel pressing against his temple, I swiftly remove my mask so he knows exactly who I am. "Did you really think you had any rights to what's mine? We might share DNA but it wasn't freely given."

Daxton has the nerve to chuckle. "Isn't everything in this fucked-up world, brother? You can't deny we're family."

I press the cold steel of the silencer tighter against his head. "I'm not denying anything. We might share blood, but we're a far cry from being family. I am, however, taking everything from you instead of the other way around. You're done, Daxton."

"Says who?" he snarls and his hand moves up as I catch a glimpse of a knife coming for my throat.

I don't blink. I don't hesitate. I do however have a pretty damn good reflex when it comes to my trigger finger. The bullet tears from the gun and enters Daxton's brain, going straight through and making the back of his head explode.

"Aw, fuck," I mutter as I stare at the wall covered with blood and brain matter.

"To whom do we have the honor?" a voice rumbles and I glance back at the screens sitting on Daxton's desk.

Fuck. I just killed a mafia boss in front of a handful of other mob bosses.

CHAPTER 12

CLOVER

"You're kidding me, right?" I gasp and stare at Hixon.

"I wish." A deep sigh rips from him as he takes a seat on the wooden table in front of me. "It was a split-second decision when I took out Daxton and I wasn't aware of the meeting he had going on with all those screens open. I should have kept him alive but that would also mean all those mafia heads were aware of Daxton being taken into custody. So, it would also defeat the purpose of having him either talk or work with the government to bring those fuckers down."

"I bet," I grumble, my mind still reeling with the flow of information Hixon just threw at me.

Holy shit. I still can't believe he gives it to me straight. My father always kept me out of the mafia business. It's why we moved to the US and the reason my brother took over. Before Hixon's information dump, he told me he wants a future with me, but he needed to be honest. Honest, because our future depends on how I handle this.

I have no freaking clue how I should take this. Hixon killed his half-brother. Yes, Daxton was about to stick a knife into him, so he didn't really have a choice with the whole self-defense–it's him or me–situation.

None of this was part of a master plan and I hate that Daxton practically forced this on Hixon. Yes, I'm taking a spin on this situation because Daxton had Hixon's father killed when he found out he was his biological father too.

Daxton is a hateful, hateful man who extorted many people around this town and thought he could force Hixon out of his ranch by making some sort of claim as an heir or something. Ugh. People truly suck and are quite insane at times.

Insane. That brings me back to the situation at hand and I sum up what Hixon just told me. "So. If I understand correctly...you're now a mob boss. Mafia. The head of the Familia because you took Daxton's place since he's your half-brother. He didn't have any other family, heirs, or whatever, and you killed him in front of all those other bosses, capos, whatever...and...how does that even work? You told me you're some consultant working for the government. Are you undercover? Is it real? How the hell would that even work?"

Hixon places his elbows on his thighs and takes his head in his hands. "Coy is practically throwing a party, spreading confetti, and buying fucking cake over the shit that happened. When he found out who saw me kill Daxton, he said I couldn't have done a better job to handle the situation and have the opportunity to bring down key players they've been after for years."

The sight before me shows a man who is dead tired, but due to the time I spent with and around him I also know he lives for this part of his job; protecting our country. One of many between the ranch, the whiskey, and help to solve cases for the government.

"Are you going to keep extorting the people in this town the way Daxton did? Keep up everything that asshole was doing? Or are you going to rule as a mafia boss in your own way?" I question.

He lifts his head and he gives me his blue eyes. "Some people will still pay for protection. There will be some crucial changes because I won't harm or fuck with innocent lives. Our main goal will be to bring down the main players, starting with Cerise Trenta. I'm giving you a choice here, Clover. I was going to be selfish by not giving you one, but with this shit happening...everything is different now. You have to be aware of the possible consequences."

"Possible consequences." I huff out a breath. "Like how my parents and brother pulled me out only to get kicked in the vagina and made a fool of by my ex? Look how well that worked out by keeping me out of the mafia world and me hooking up with a 'normal' guy. I might have been pulled back in but maybe it's inevitable. I love it here. The horses, the ranch, your boys, you. I get to read a book, cook, enjoy the sunrise, and sundown, ride and take care of horses, try cocktails with the whiskey you guys make…even if you think I should appreciate the fine taste instead of diluting it with other liquids."

This gets me a twitch of his sexy lips, exactly how I knew it would make him laugh.

I reach out to take his hand. "What I'm trying to say is…my parents wanted different things for me. My brother did too. My ex? He definitely wanted to change me. You? You're laying it all out, telling me the things we can't change. Basically, giving me the choice in all of it. A choice I don't need because I can't leave. I made up my mind before you so much as told me I was yours. Hell, I completely sidetracked you when you didn't want to hire me."

He reaches out to cup my face. "This is different, though. You'll be pulled back into this world and will be known as mine. There's a risk they might want to take me out. I'm not hiding and they are very aware of my past work with the government. Only Coy is our contact and everything else is behind closed doors so no one knows we're still on their payroll."

I shrug. "At the end of the day, all that matters is our state of mind and wellbeing. Which means I love it here, along with the company."

Adoration fills his features and he cups the side of my head stroking his thumb along my cheek as sadness suddenly flashes in his eyes.

"What's wrong?" I question, instantly knowing there's something he hasn't shared yet.

"One of the mafia bosses who witnessed that shit?"

I swallow hard, afraid of the thought that goes through my head by the way he looks at me. I bob my head for him to continue, but I already know what he's going to say.

"Was your brother."

"Are you going to take him down too?" I croak.

My brother and I cut ties for a reason when my parents took me to the US. He wanted me out of that world where I would have been pawned off into an arranged marriage. Hell, I have a niece who just turned eighteen whom I've never met and I'm sure he needs to marry her off soon as well.

"You're the only one I shared it with and shut down the feed before anyone else rounded the desk. The government isn't aware and as far as I know, he's also not on their radar since he's out of our jurisdiction."

"But you are going after him?" I press.

He keeps staring at me as he gives it to me straight. "I don't know. Like I said, he isn't on their radar so if he keeps his shit where he is there won't be any issue."

I give him a tight nod. "Thank you for your honesty."

"Always," he instantly replies.

The corners of my mouth tick up. I wasn't lying when I told him everything here makes me happy. The ranch, the animals, the work, but mostly it's him. The sex is amazing, his honesty and directness are a part of it as well.

This man knows what he wants and isn't afraid to give the black and white tiny letters to make sure you're aware of all the bad along with the good. No pretty picture was painted. Nope, he throws raw necessities at my feet to make something less perfect together, a realistic vision of a shared future.

"I'm in," I firmly tell him. "Always, for everything. You and I. No secrets, no lies, no bullshit."

He takes my face in both hands to pull me up and places his lips a breath away from mine. "No secrets, no lies, no bullshit. You and I. Together. Always," he echoes and takes my mouth in a scorching kiss.

No regrets. We should have added that because even if life is shitty and there will be a load of havoc coming our way, this right here…being in his huge, warm, capable, and loving hands is where I feel safe and treasured.

"I thought you two were going to discuss shit?" Shepherd remarks from somewhere else in the room.

I gasp and take a step back to glare at him. "Didn't your father teach you to knock? Because I'm pretty sure we closed and locked that door."

Shepherd shrugs. "I'm the underboss now, I don't need to knock."

Rolling my eyes, I mutter, "Really? Are you already doing the whole traditional structure? Let me guess." I jerk my thumb over my shoulder. "Romer is this boss' consigliere, huh?"

Shepherd grins and I have my answer.

He sobers quickly and slides his attention to his father. "Hate to interrupt you and the wifey, but…I gotta leave to pick up my future wifey from the airport."

"What?" I gasp in outrage. "How can you be engaged when I haven't even seen you with a woman since I got here? Why didn't you say anything?"

Shepherd shrugs and I swing my gaze to Hixon to catch the man cringing.

"What's going on?" I demand.

"Daxton owed Trenta a blood debt. With me killing my half-brother Trenta demands I take over and with it is holding the past agreement to tie our families. He was sending his daughter off for an arranged marriage. I told him I'm already spoken for, but he still demanded a husband for his daughter to make sure our families are tied. If we refused–"

"Both sides would lose and there would be war and all that mafia bullshit," I finish his statement for him. "What a bunch of alpha-hole dicks."

"Yeah, so…anyway. I'm going to pick up my lovely wife-to-be. She's of age and a total knock-out. I've been told she's a great cook as well. Now,

128 A Clyden's Ranch Wiseguys novella

be sure to keep your lips sealed when you're around her since she's the enemy and all." He shoots me a wink and strolls out the door whistling.

I whip my head in Hixon's direction. "Is he for real? Does he even understand the commitment? This girl…this woman…how old is she exactly? If she's raised in this world she's still a virgin and has been kept out of mafia business to be a housewife, arm candy, a mother. Hence the cooking. Oh. My. Freaking. Gosh. You idiots." I jab my finger against Hixon's chest. "It's a good thing I decided to stick around because you idiots are going to ruin things before you can even bring down one damn mob boss."

Hixon chuckles and his arm flashes out to wrap around my waist.

Pulling me flush against his body he tells me, "You're the perfect woman for me. Already running this house with your sharp tongue. We need you to keep things straight and real, as well as keep an eye on the intruder whom we don't know. She might be a spy, but on the other hand, she was already on the plane here when her father switched husbands on her. The woman might be caught in the middle. The things we've learned so far from Trenta aren't… women friendly so to speak."

I swallow hard, knowing how different the world is from what I was born in. My family didn't want that from me, other traditional families, though? Let's just say I consider myself lucky to have been blessed with parents like mine.

"We just have to be careful," I tell him. "Knowledge is power and keeps us on our toes. It's also why I value your honesty."

Hixon places his forehead against mine. "You're too good for me."

I grin. "Keep giving me those orgasms and I'll consider us even."

He barks out a laugh and something in this room whines. My eyes go wide and I take a step back to look around me.

"What was that?" I whisper.

Hixon chuckles and rounds his desk to scoop something up. He's suddenly holding a large, white, and fluffy bundle.

"Awwww," I coo and feel a lump fill my throat as Hixon places a puppy into my arms.

"I found him in one of the back rooms of Daxton's house. He was in a kennel. Sonny found a full-grown white shepherd out back that was shot in the head. He thinks this little one was bought to replace the old one as a guard dog. There was no one to take care of him and you did mention wanting a dog." He shrugs. "He needs to be trained, though. Maybe we could still check if there's an older dog we can adopt as a buddy."

I shove my nose into the soft fur and try to hide my happy tears. "Thank you," I croak. "He's perfect."

"You're perfect," Hixon grunts. "And all mine."

I blink through the wetness clinging to my lashes. "All yours," I full-heartedly agree.

EPILOGUE
One year later

HIXON

I lean back to bring Witness to a stop. We've just herded the other horses to put them into the other pasture for today. I give a sharp whistle and Des, our white shepherd, comes rushing toward me. He's a little over a year old now and is a perfect guard dog who also likes to work with me when I'm herding the horses.

Sonny comes to a stop next to me and jerks his chin in the direction of the stables. "Your woman is practically glowing holding that baby while she undresses you with her eyes." He chuckles and shakes his head. "Dismount and give me the reins. I'll put Witness in his stable for you."

I keep my eye on my woman and I don't need to check because I know she's happy as fuck. I do exactly what Sonny says and tell him, "Thanks, man.

I'll see you tomorrow morning. Nine sharp, don't forget."

"The meeting, yeah, I know. Tomorrow," he grunts and I dismiss him to head for my woman.

I grab the fence and jump over, earning my woman's gaze to turn heated as she's holding the little one firmly in her arms.

"You look good holding a baby," I huskily tell her.

Des plunks his ass near Clover's feet and leans his body against her leg, earning him a scratch behind his ear from her.

A sexy as fuck chuckle slips past my woman's lips. "I still, to this day, cannot believe you gave me babies."

Now I'm the one chuckling.

"Well, not you specifically, but I still get to hold, love, spoil, smell, and do all the fun things. The most fun part is returning the baby to the parents. Perks. Definitely huge freaking perks."

I brush my thumb over the little one's forehead. "Definitely," I murmur.

"Hey," Shepherd quips and carefully takes his kid from Clover. "I was looking for this little one." His eyes find mine. "Remember, we have a meeting tomorrow morning."

"I just reminded Sonny." I jerk my chin in the direction of the little bundle he's holding. "You should be the one being reminded if you have another sleepless night."

Shepherd leans in to brush his nose against the top of his baby's head. "I'll be there."

He turns and stalks off. Clover steps closer and wraps her arms around my waist. I cup the back of her head and pull her close.

"See? We don't have the commitment of all those sleepless nights. We can offer to babysit and give them a break, but all the responsibilities are on them." Her head tips back so she can look me in the eye. "Seriously, Hixon. I never dreamed of all the things in life you fill to the brim. I lucked out the day I met you."

"Fill to the brim, huh? Like my cock filling your pussy so far up your little, curvy body that the tip of it kisses your cervix?"

She rolls her eyes. "Your head is always in the gutter. One would think an old man doesn't have the stamina to keep his young wife fully sated, but I guess I got lucky in that department too."

"I'm the lucky one," I murmur and hoist her up, carrying her straight into the house.

She giggles and I never get tired of hearing the enticing sound. What I love more are the moans that slip over her lips when I tunnel in and out of her body. The way she huskily croaks my name when I eat her pussy.

Not a day goes by when I'm not thankful she's in my life. A solid part of who I am, what we do, and where we're going. Shit still gets hard at times, and yes, we do have our issues, disagreement, and fights, but we are also a solid team.

I stalk right into our bedroom and kick the door shut with my boot. I carefully place her on the bed and love the dress she's wearing. Though, it is in my way and obstructing my vision of her gorgeous body. I throw my Stetson on the nearby desk and grab the hem of my shirt to pull it over my head.

"Dress. Off," I order and reach for my belt.

She kicks off her boots and scrambles up to get rid of her dress. Another thing I love about our connection; mutual lust spiking the chemistry between us. One might think it might fade a bit over time and we might have only spent one year together, and yet it grows stronger each and every day.

I shove my jeans down along with my boxers, letting my cock spring free. My sack is heavy with the need to release and her lust-filled gaze is almost my undoing when she licks her lips at the sight of my throbbing cock. Palming myself, I squeeze and slowly stroke up and down. She follows the movement and leans forward, licking the bead of precum right from the slit.

"Fuck," I hiss and shove my fingers into her hair to fist it and keep her in place. "Open your mouth and suck my cock."

Her greedy mouth opens and she gives me her cum-begging eyes. This woman. She has me wrapped around her finger and kneeling at her feet to worship her in every damn way. My heart belongs to her the way our souls are merged together.

Age is a mere number while feelings shared and lives lived are what make the blood pump through our hearts. You aren't living if you stick to the shade normal people like to blind your eyes with.

We live our lives the way we want to live. Balancing the right side of the law while throwing some outlaws into the mix as well. There can't be good without the bad, the darkness without the blinding light, and life bleeding into death.

But as long as my heart beats it will be due to the rhythm of this woman's love. She gives me all and I gladly return the favor. I tighten my fist and pull her away from my cock, making the limb fall from her lips with a soft plop.

"I'm going to fuck you now. Take that sweet pussy that belongs to me. Only me," I fiercely growl.

It might have been a year, but I still feel the need to remind her who she exactly belongs to. Besides, I know for a fact she instantly gets wet when I give her those words. Like now. She moans and lays back on the bed, legs falling apart, allowing me the room to work with.

I grab her knees and push them further apart and up toward her head. Pussy in the air and wide open for me as I lean in and taste her. Pure heaven. I rub my beard against the inside of her thighs, knowing she likes to feel the burn.

She moans and begs me to fuck her. Taking my time to lick and suck her sweet pussy, I finally give in and reach down to palm my cock. Scooting closer

I slide the mushroom head through her slick lips, making sure to bump her clit each and every time. Raising her hips she tries to catch my cock with her wet heat. So impatient.

I tease her two more times and then dive home. Her spine curls, lips part in a silent scream and she's fucking beautiful as she takes my cock. I grip her curvy hips and start to slam my hips forward, filling her, almost pulling out to leave the tip in and fuck right back in.

My cock is slick with her juices, pussy lips stretch around my thick length; the perfect visual of our bodies connected. This right here is the bonus points in life. The cherry on top of the fucking-cake because life is all about waking up together in the same bed, having breakfast, spending time, fulfilling dreams, and making sure to take and give pleasure while we're at it.

Her orgasm catches both of us by surprise and she comes with a loud groan. "Hixoooooooooon."

Damn. I love the extended version of my name spilling from her lips. My cock is being treated with some mighty tight waves and it's enough to pull me under her spell. I manage to thrust three more times before I'm rooted deep.

Cum rips from me, spraying her insides and I groan loudly as I throw her name in the mix of it as well. My energy is drained and I crash forward. Pulling her close to me, I roll over so I'm now lying on my back with her draped over me. Yeah, a way better position.

She snuggles close, her breath fanning out on my skin. There's been one question roaming through my head for about a year now. I was sure back then and had something made special. Except somehow, it's never the right moment.

Brushing my lips against the crown of her head I murmur, "Marry me."

Her head whips up so damn fast that she snags me on the chin and I barely manage to swallow a curse.

"What? she gasps and brushes her fingers over the top of her head.

I rub my chin. "You heard me."

"Yes." She bobs her head making relief pour through my veins until she adds, "I heard you."

"Motherfucker," I mutter and the mischief in her gaze lets me know she did it on fucking purpose.

I flip our bodies and have her pinned underneath me when I growl, "Tell me you will."

"I will." The corner of her mouth twitches.

"Will what?" I demand.

She rolls her eyes, probably checking if she still has a functioning brain cell because I'm fucking doubting it the way she's pushing me.

"I will marry you, Hixon. I love you. There's no doubt in my mind. This." She places her hand on my chest, right over my heart. "This is where I belong."

"Yeah, you do," I huskily tell her.

I crawl off the bed and reach for my jeans to take

my keys from my pocket. Her eyes go wide when I take the ring from the tiny brown leather pouch I have attached to it. Taking her hand, I slide the ring on her finger. She gasps and stares up at me. Tears of happiness fill her gorgeous eyes.

I cup the side of her face and tell her, "You're my lifeblood, the spark of electricity that fires up life itself. The day we crossed paths was when I became complete. If I would have given this to you a year ago it would have been too soon. We're still barely starting but our future has always been wide open. It's why I want to continue living as man and wife… because I fucking love you so damn much."

She laughs on a sob and throws her arms around me to pull me close. "I love you too. So. Damn. Much. You make me happy," she whispers. "So. Damn. Happy."

"Me too, wifey. Me too," I fiercely tell her.

Like I said; we're barely starting out and I can't wait to experience what lies ahead in the future we'll ride in together, as man and wife, from here on out.

THANK YOU!

Thank you for reading Hixon's story. Can't get enough? Shepherd's story is next. Here's the link to all the information about the standalone Clyden's Ranch series:
https://books2read.com/rl/ClydensRanchWiseguys

If you love to read other Cowboy stories by me…I have a whole Cowboy Bikers MC world filled with standalone novellas waiting for you to dive in: **https://books2read.com/rl/cowboybikersmc**

Be sure to check out all my other MC, Mafia, Paranormal MC, and Contemporary Romance series!
https://books2read.com/rl/EstherESchmidt

Signup for Esther's newsletter:
https://esthereschmidt.nl/newsletter

A Clyden's Ranch Wiseguys novella

SPECIAL THANKS

My beta team; Lynne, Tammi, Wendy,
my pimp team, and to you, as my reader…
Thanks so much! You guys rock!

Contact:

I love hearing from my readers.

Email:

authoresthereschmidt@gmail.com

Or contact my PA **Christi Durbin**
for any questions you might have.
facebook.com/CMDurbin

Visit Esther E. Schmidt online:

Website:
www.esthereschmidt.nl

Facebook - AuthorEstherESchmidt
Twitter - @esthereschmidt
Instagram - @esthereschmidt
Pinterest - @esthereschmidt

Signup for Esther's newsletter:
esthereschmidt.nl/newsletter

Join Esther's fan group on Facebook:
www.facebook.com/groups/estherselite

MORE BOOKS

A Clyden's Ranch Wiseguys novella

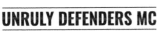

Printed in Great Britain
by Amazon